Praise for **Duets:**

"***DUETS**... a very intriguing and somewhat sad story. A story of lovers separated by fate. When they meet again, sparks fly, but this story is not a fairy tale romance. This is more like real life, and made my heart hurt a little.* —Long and Short reviews.

Praise for **Molly Harper:**

"***MOLLY HARPER** ...is the first book I've read by this author, but it won't be my last! Ms. Gamble does a wonderful job of drawing these characters and making them just leap off the page."* —Long and Short Reviews

"*I rarely gush over a book these days. I read at least one, sometimes two books a day and so I can be hard to move. But, this one really got to me... you do not want to miss... **MOLLY HARPER**."* —Clue Review.

Praise for **Secret Sister**:

"*Along with being a very unique and captivating plot, **SECRET SISTER** offers a shocking turn of the paranormal kind. So if you are the type of person that wants ordinary romance in a book, you won't find that here. This is a story of friendship, family, and most of all, true love and what those things can mean. I cannot recommend **SECRET SISTER** strongly enough"* —Fresh Fiction, Fresh Reviews.

december wedding

Emelle Gamble

Love to dearest Yvonne — my heroine xxx Emelle

Posh Publishing, USA

Copyright © 2014 by Posh Publishing, USA

This is a work of fiction. Names, characters, places and incidents are the product of the author's imagination or are used fictitiously. Any resemblance to actual events, locales or persons, living or dead, is purely coincidental.

Posh Publishing/published by arrangement with the author

"DECEMBER WEDDING" by Emelle Gamble, Copyright © 2014 by Emelle Gamble

All rights reserved. Excerpt as permitted under the U.S. Copyright Act of 1976, no part of this publication may be reproduced, distributed, or transmitted in any form or by any means, or stored in a database or retrieval system, without the prior written permission of the author.

ISBN: 150339591X

Cover design © Tammy Seidick Design
Formatting by Anessa Books

dedication

With love to our beautiful daughter–in–law, Heidi Jo Nuccio, who has claimed a place in our hearts forever.

acknowledgments

Thank you to...

Junis Cariello for her thoughtful, helpful and generous time and help.

Janna Shay for her expert and insightful copy editing work.

Meredith Bond for her calm, professional assistance in all things formatting.

And, as so many times before, thank you to the talented and artistic Tammy Seidick for her gorgeous cover work and support in all areas of electronic marketing.

Babes, every one.

chapter one

Molly Harper lay beside Cruz Morales in their darkened bedroom as the familiar night sounds floated in on the Santa Barbara breezes.

She was on her second set of counting backwards from one hundred, trying to fall asleep. *Forty–two, forty–one...*

"Will you marry me?" Cruz asked, his voice husky and close.

"No." Her pulse jumped, even though he had asked her this every night since last Christmas Eve. In the beginning, saying no had been easy. Meaning it was getting more difficult.

"Why not?" Cruz pressed.

"You know why not. I love you too much to subject you to a media feeding frenzy over our plans, or to see you deal with being called '*Mr. Molly Harper*' the rest of your life."

"The wedding thing won't be that big a deal. And I'll just knock any man who calls me that on his ass, *chica*." His tone was joking.

She didn't laugh. "Yet another reason my answer is no. I'm an actress whose life attracts the press like a bush of honeysuckle attracts bees. And bees sting. I am not having us turned into a cheap headline again. Remember my divorce?" The scandalous story of her ex–husband's affair, which ended their marriage, poked at a sore spot in her heart. "I'm not up to that kind of publicity, Cruz. Especially now."

She rubbed her heavily pregnant belly. "Good night."

"We could get married at the courthouse in Taos, or at your house there. We could keep it a secret. People can have a wedding the same day they get the license in New Mexico. I checked."

He checked?

Molly sighed and turned to face him. "A secret? You know how unlikely that is. Someone at the courthouse would snap a photo and text their friend, or send it to *People Magazine*, and those folks would tweet it to fifty thousand of their closest followers."

"Are you sure we're still that interesting? The public seems more into royal babies and Mrs. George Clooney lately."

"Right. That's why there were only two *paparazzi* outside the restaurant where we ate last Friday." *They were always there*, she thought with a pang. Her brain reran snippets of some of the heartbreaking events from the last two years of her life, recorded and forever available on the internet.

Cruz struggling to recover from the motorcycle accident that nearly killed him.

Her movie star husband leaving her for another woman. Her ex and the other woman having a baby.

Mother's death.

All played out on the front pages of newspapers and websites around the world.

A rattling breath escaped through her lips. "Let's just stay under the radar for a while longer. I don't need to be married to know you love me."

In the midnight shadows, his generous mouth softened against the hard curves of his face. "I do love you. I've always loved you. Even when we were apart."

"Thank you for that," she whispered. "And for coming back to me."

"I couldn't stay away." Cruz touched her nose with his finger and cleared his throat, which he did when he recited a favorite poem, another bedtime habit.

"*i carry your heart with me (i carry it in my heart) i am never without it (anywhere I go you go,*

*my dear; and whatever is done by only me is your
doing, my darling) i fear
no fate (for you are my fate, my sweet) i want
no world (for beautiful you are my world, my
true)."*

Molly's eyes burned. "I hope you don't sound that sexy when you recite love poetry in class, Professor. All those hot coeds will be trying to jump your bones."

"That one is just for you, Molly. I read e.e. cummings when I was recovering in the hospital. He brought you back to me."

"Oh please," she whispered. "No more talking about those horrible times."

"Why? They don't matter now; they hardly mattered then. I mean, once we got back together, the past was gone."

"The past is never gone. It lives forever on *Facebook* and *Google*."

"No one looks at those things."

That made her laugh, as she knew he had hoped it would.

Molly embraced him through the smooth silk of the sheets and then rolled onto her other side.

Cruz spooned his body against hers, his hand resting gently on her hip. "You feel like heaven, warm and round and all mine." He kissed her neck.

"I am all yours. Now, no more talking. Harry and Jackson are getting married in less than a week. I need my beauty sleep."

He gently rubbed her stomach. "It's not possible for you to be more beautiful than you are now."

"Thank heaven that's not true." Molly chuckled. "I also have that interview run–through tomorrow. I need to rest so I don't look like I've pulled an all–nighter."

"You're going ahead with it, then?" Dismay was clear in his tone.

"Yes. The movie needs publicity before its released next month. And this Diane Kinsey, the journalist I agreed to talk to, is a rising star." Celia Kent, her publicist, was very protective of who she let interview Molly. The actress thought about Celia for a moment; thankfully she trusted the young woman's judgment as much as her own. "How do you feel about my telling the world you are the father of my baby?"

"I thought you were keeping that private. It's no one's business but ours."

"I know." She nestled closer to him. "But the public likes to know about babies and happy stuff. And you and I having a baby is great news. So I think we can share a little info, and still keep it on our terms."

"The life of a movie star really isn't her own," Cruz said softly. He kissed her neck, pressing himself against her. "Whatever you want to do is fine with me."

Molly leaned her head back, inviting more attention. His mouth found the lobe of her ear as his hand moved to her breast.

Her breathe quickened as he gently caressed her swollen nipple. "It's not fair to kiss me like this when I can't do much about it."

"We'll make up for that soon enough."

"Ha. Not as soon as you're hoping, I think." She rolled onto her back, her body moving awkwardly, but she needed a real kiss. Molly slid her arms around Cruz's neck and pulled him closer.

Passion flared in his dark eyes as he kissed her deeply, before reluctantly letting her go. "Go to sleep, *madrecita*." He rubbed his hand once more across her stomach. "*Buenas noches pequeno bebe.*"

After a few moments, Cruz began to gently snore, though his arm stayed possessively around her.

Molly closed her eyes. Things between her and Cruz were so good at this moment. So perfect. She was blessed with most of what she had ever wanted and prayed for, but she was often consumed with anxiety instead of joy.

She did not share this with Cruz, because she could not explain the reasons for it. All she knew was that her present bounty of blessings often left her feeling fearful and undeserving. Cruz was not easy to rattle, but if she told him how she felt, she knew he would push her to see more doctors.

He had stood by her, calmly and logically talking her down to earth through the harrowing touch–and–go first trimester, and a worrisome second full of more medical tests and consults. If he knew how terrified she still was that something might go wrong, despite all the doctors assuring her everything was normal, he would think she was crazy.

"*Chica loca*," he teasingly commented in the past. But if he thought she was really suffering, he would do more than tease. He would insist she see a psychiatrist.

Which is the last thing I feel like doing now, with so much going on. Molly squeezed her eyes closed tighter. *Maybe I am loca. If only Mother was here.*

Her thoughts shifted to Norma Wintz, the woman who adopted her when she was a newborn and raised her as her natural child. She had always known when Molly was worried and managed to defuse the fears, at least a little, by listening and talking her through them.

When Norma died, she and Molly had overcome the damage from the secrets and lies that had been revealed about the circumstances of Molly's birth.

I still miss her every day.

Tears bubbled in Molly's eyes as she gave into grief for a moment. She kept her breathing even and let them leak out and dry against her hair. Cruz moved restlessly, as if her distress got through to him even as he slept.

Gently she moved his arm and rolled back onto her side, pushing a pillow under her belly.

She glanced at the bedside clock. It was after 2 a.m.

I need to sleep.

The baby kicked and Molly's abdomen tightened. Her kidneys felt uncomfortably full, even though she had been to

december wedding

the bathroom a half hour ago. She lay still and focused on Cruz's even breathing.

Molly drifted fitfully off to sleep, praying she could manage the stress and keep her anxiety from getting any worse in the few weeks she had left to her pregnancy.

# # #

"Thank you for doing this interview with me, Molly. I appreciate it. I know you don't do many sit–downs with the press."

"You have a reputation for fairness," the movie actress replied. She smiled at Diane Kinsey, *Tonight Magazine's* newest journalist. "And I appreciate you coming to me for the interview." Molly gestured at the sky above her shaded patio in Santa Barbara, California. "Natural lighting always flatters, I think. And it's nice not to have to travel to your New York studios."

"Hey, we'd go anywhere to talk to you." The reporter was sleek and racehorse pretty, with glittering green eyes. "You look gorgeous, by the way. That whole 'pregnant women glow' thing is true in your case."

"Thank you. Right now I'm feeling like a water balloon with feet." Molly rested her hands gently on her stomach. "Don't be alarmed if I suddenly run for the bathroom."

"Kidney kicks from the little one, right? I remember that when I was pregnant. But I never looked as good as you do now."

"I've got professional make–up people everywhere."

"I need their number." Diane turned to her producer, Phil, a bearded young man in a faded Nirvana tee shirt. "We good to start?"

"Any time you're ready, Diane," he replied. His camera operator nodded and the sound technician, a young woman with blue streaks in her hair, held up a huge microphone.

Molly folded her hands in her lap. She did not feel as comfortable as she had hoped she would with this broadcaster, who struck her as a touch fake, but then, she was never at ease doing interviews.

emelle gamble

"This is rehearsal film which we won't use for the on–air broadcast, Molly. I want to get a feel for how to converse with you, keep it natural and pace the questions, which I'm sure will be full of some you're sick of answering. I just want you to feel comfortable with me. Okay?"

"Okay." Molly smiled and looked around the patio. There was no sign of Cruz. She smiled bigger. His presence made her nervous when she was working.

"I am going to hold some questions back for the final interview, too, if that's okay. I want your reactions to be fresh."

Molly caught Celia's eye. Her publicist had assured her Diane knew the topics not to bring up...her prior marriage to actor Ben Delmonico and his love affair with Miss Universe being the biggest.

"Ask away," Molly said.

Diane's voice dropped. "I understand post–production work on your last movie is finished. We hear it's going to be released by the end of the year."

"Yes, final editing was completed a couple of weeks ago. Previews will start December first. One more thing I can give thanks for this year."

"So it will be in theatres Christmas week?"

"Fingers crossed." Molly made the gesture with her hand.

"How difficult was it being the lead actress, as well as one of the producers on that film?"

"I was busier than I've ever been before on a set, but I enjoyed it. The amount of decisions that have to be made on a daily basis by producers is staggering. Catering. Contracts. Location permits." She shook her head. "It gave me a new appreciation for what it takes to make a movie."

"There's some speculation that both you and your two co–stars will be nominated for Academy Awards. You've already won, once. Are you excited by the buzz?"

december wedding

"I'm thrilled the public is looking forward to see it." Molly beamed. "Did you read the book the movie was based on?"

"Couldn't put it down. I'm a sucker for set-ups like that one. Car crash. Two best friends. Woo-woo paranormal body and soul transfer." Diane laughed. "Really made me wonder if my husband would know me if everything about me changed."

"I liked that best about the movie, that it gives the audience a chance to wonder, *what would I do?*"

"And it had all those secrets, the family ones and those between the women who thought they knew everything about each other."

"None of us know everything about each other."

"Which is just how you like it, right Molly?"

The question made her pause. She wrung her hands together, keeping her face relaxed. "Yes. I do like to keep some things private. Don't you?"

"I don't expect to, being in the public eye. Do you?"

"No. But hope springs eternal."

Diane laughed unconvincingly. "Let me ask a few more things about your new movie. Do you think it would have been a stronger film if the original cast had stayed in place?"

Despite her best effort, Molly's face stiffened. Her ex and the woman he left her for were originally cast in the film opposite her. But when the cheating scandal broke, Molly refused to do the movie until it was recast. Diane surely knew all of this. "No. I don't think anyone could have done a better job than Mila and Ryan. Things turned out as they were meant to, I think."

"Those two are hot. That's for sure." The journalist's eyes lowered to Molly's midsection. "So what's next for you? When's your baby due?"

Molly's hand moved a fraction higher, instinctively trying to shield her unborn child from the press's interest in its existence, even before it took its first breath. "Late January. However, let me stop you here. I don't want to answer any more questions about the baby, okay? Don't ask me the sex, or name, or any of that. I'm trying to give my child a little privacy, at least until it's here."

"But the baby of an Oscar–winner is always born under the limelight. Surely you know that?" the newswoman replied.

Across the room, Celia stood up, the look on her face making it clear she was ready to close down the interview. Molly caught Celia's eye and shook her head slightly. The publicist sat back down.

"I do know that," Molly said. "But you're a mom, Diane. I am sure you understand I want to cut down the glare as much as I can. At least until the kid can say 'back off' to anyone getting too close."

Diane nodded. "I hear you. I'm sure this baby's mom and dad will be right there, helping run us pesky media types off. Which brings me to my next subject. Cruz Morales. Rumor has it you two long–time friends are getting married next week, right here in Santa Barbara." Diane waved her hand at the spacious patio behind the house where Molly had grown up. "It's a perfect setting for a wedding, in my opinion."

"I'm not getting married next week. Or anytime in the foreseeable future," Molly replied quickly. "Your sources are mistaken."

"Really? We've got several who swear the catering, flowers, and a certain top–flight singer are booked for a wedding the Friday after Thanksgiving."

"Nope. All I am hosting a week from Friday is a small family get–together. Not my wedding."

"Is Lana Del Rey singing at your 'family get–together'?"

"Let it go, Diane," Celia said, appearing beside the journalist. "Molly doesn't comment about private events. You know that. And you know how she feels about the press covering non–show business friends. Professor Morales and family are off limits."

"I'd say Professor Morales is certainly more than a friend." The newswoman arched her skinny eyebrows at Molly. "Isn't he the father of your child?"

Molly locked glances with Diane for a moment before letting a grin slowly bloom over her face. "Well, since you asked so *nicely*, Diane. Yes. Professor Cruz Morales is the father of my child."

Molly heard Celia gasp as a murmur rolled around the patio. All those present realized Diane had just been handed some big news.

The journalist pointed at her producer. "Did Larry get that, Phil?"

"He did." The producer's voice sounded excited. "We've got a headline now, Miss Harper. And while we've agreed we can't use this pre–interview film, will you say the same thing if we ask you on–air?"

"Yes."

"And you'll keep this exclusive to me, Molly, until we air?" Diane asked. "I will be forever grateful."

"Yes, of course." She tilted her chin up at the woman opposite her. "Ask that question in the final interview, but I don't want any follow–up on if we're going to get married, how Cruz is doing, health–wise, or if he's fully recovered his speech. And no reference to the motorcycle accident that almost killed him, or his recovery."

"But your fans are interested in those issues."

"I understand people want to know about my life, but I want to keep the information I share to be primarily about my movies. They are curious about me, which I accept, but that right of curiosity does not extend to Cruz. He's not in show business."

"Are you two getting married any time soon? Off the record," Diane added.

"*No*. I thought I just made that clear."

"You did, but I had to ask one more time." Diane grinned. "You and Ben Delmonico churned the tabloids for months, so I can understand not wanting to give the press another opening to rehash that scandal."

"I'm glad you understand." Molly's voice was strained. "Can we move on?"

"Absolutely."

Diane asked a series of questions about Molly's tentative next project in development, a romance about a career woman, her estranged husband, and the ghost of a famous movie star.

"The biggest problem is finding someone to play Cary Grant," Molly said. "He's the definition of inimitable."

"That's for sure." Diane leaned closer. "Are you going back to work next year, after your baby is born?"

"I'm going to take a few months to look at scripts. Interview with possible directors, co-stars. But I wouldn't expect to do any filming for a year or two."

"How does Cruz feel about that? It's well known he doesn't love what you do."

"No comment." Molly let her smile fade. "Remember?"

"Are you thinking of retiring from acting? We've heard some whispers about that."

Molly twitched. She needed to pee. "No. All I'm thinking of at this time is going to the ladies room." She stood and winked at Phil. "No letting Larry follow me in there, okay?"

"Never," the producer said quickly. "Even we have limits."

"Not sure I believe *that*, Phil." The people on the patio each laughed with varying degrees of irony as Molly headed for the house.

"Okay, fifteen minutes, everyone," Celia barked. "Molly, can I see you for a few minutes in the den?" The publicist followed her boss inside.

"Are you sure you want to let Diane run with the 'Cruz–is–the–father' story?" Celia asked. "You know that even if she doesn't include references to his accident, and how long it took him to get his memory and speech back, other media certainly will be pushing it."

december wedding

"I know. But the longer I keep Cruz out of the picture with the baby, the bigger the story will be when a photographer catches him pushing the stroller. I'm hoping it will diffuse their interest a little." Molly frowned. "I really need to pee."

"Okay. You want something to eat?"

"Yes." She thought for a second. "How about a half of a peanut butter sandwich and some tea."

"I'll get it." Celia hurried off.

Molly headed for her bedroom suite in the sprawling Hacienda-style house she had lived at most of the summers of her life. Inside, she locked the bathroom door and shook her head at how ridiculous her life was, that she had to do that in her own home.

A couple of minutes later, she washed her hands and stared at herself in the mirror. Her hair, famous tousled blonde locks casually styled, looked good. And though her makeup had been applied professionally for the interview, she looked tired. She had dark circles and a pinched look to her mouth.

It's worry. With a sigh, she freshened her lipstick, checked her teeth for smudges, yanked on her blouse, which was gaping open because of her huge mommy-to-be boobs, and walked back outdoors.

Celia and Artie Stein, her attorney, were huddled by the walkway to the pool. "Molly, can I have a word?" Artie asked.

"Hey, you." She gave the burly lawyer a hug. "You decided to come watch after all?"

"Hey yourself, beautiful. Yeah, I wanted to be sure this Diane person understands her contract. You get a final look-see at the tape at least forty-eight hours before it airs. We don't have edit approval, but at least we'll be forewarned and can push back before it airs, if we have to."

"Thanks, Artie."

"You're welcome. Where's Cruz?" His eyes darted around the assembled technicians. "Inside?"

"No. He and Marta took Jesse to the beach."

"Good." Artie visibly relaxed that the man who was known for being volatile around the press was not present. "Celia said the warm-up is going good, but you have to be careful of that one." He jerked his glance to Diane, busy on her phone across the patio. "She's known for asking innocent questions that drag people down a hole they have trouble digging out of."

"That's why I gave her the scoop." Molly rubbed her belly and stretched. "She'll relax a little, now that she's got a headline."

"I'm surprised she's heard about the wedding," Celia whispered. "I had all the vendors sign non-disclosure agreements, and the flower guy doesn't even know it's your house they're going to. I'm picking them up."

"Don't worry about it," Molly said. "Harry and Jackson deserve their privacy, but they understood this might happen." She shrugged her shoulders. "I probably shouldn't have agreed to host it here at the house, but I love Harry and knew he wanted to have it near his brother and Anne. He won't mind if someone reports they had a wedding at a movie star's house." She giggled. "He'll probably get a kick out of it."

"Well yeah, but what if someone finds out Harry is your half-brother?"

Artie kept his voice low, but Molly flinched. They all stared at Diane, who was furiously texting.

When Molly met her birth mother, Anne Sullivan, and her two half-brothers for the first time last year, she had vowed not to share with the public. She turned to Artie. "I don't see how or why my relationship with the Sullivans would come out. Harry has not told anyone I am his half-sister, and neither has Jackson. He has not even told his parents yet. As for Anne, she'd die before she'd say a word. Remember, she never even told her own sons until she told me. I think this is one part of my private life I'll be able to keep private."

Celia blinked behind her huge black-framed glasses. It was clear she was not as optimistic. "How are you getting along with Anne?"

"Pretty well, I think. We are taking it slow but I think our getting to know each other is working. She's certainly not trying to replace Mother." Molly inhaled. "But then, no one could replace Norma. She was a force of nature."

Artie and Celia nodded. "I miss her every time I'm here," Celia said softly.

Molly squeezed her shoulder. "Me, too. Okay, let's wrap this up. Diane and her crew will be back tomorrow at noon. Make sure my makeup goddess, JoJo, shows up here by ten, Celia. Despite her best efforts this morning, I think I look about fifty today." She touched her face. "Ask her to bring extra foundation. And a trowel."

The three laughed. Molly gave Artie a hug, and then walked with Celia back to the chair in the center of the slate patio.

"Remember, if any question feels intrusive, you don't have to answer." Celia squeezed Molly's arm. "And you don't look tired. You look stunning and so happy."

"I am happy."

"You deserve to be." The usually cryptic young woman's eyes welled up.

"Remind me to give you a raise, Celia." Molly smiled and settled back into the interview hot seat. "And don't worry about me. I can handle Diane Kinsey."

chapter two

Cruz drove up to Molly's family home, through the security gate and onto the wide drive. He parked his old pick-up at the far end and scowled. The network news truck and two sleek foreign cars sat empty in the spaces for visitors, which meant the journalist was still interviewing Molly.

No valen los buitres, he swore under his breath. He slammed the truck's door and walked to the back entrance beside the sprawling main house.

Molly needs her rest, and she's doing this stupid interview to help the studio. She needs to relax. She's worrying all the time now, I know it.

Cruz knew from loving the woman for the last twenty years, that journalists were as interested in picking over the details of her private life as they were in her movies.

Worthless vultures, he thought, damning them in a second language. Cruz opened the wrought-iron gate and walked along the side of the garage.

"Hello, Dr. Morales," a woman called out.

Cruz stopped and looked to his right. In the side yard at a small teak table where the gardener did the potting, a dark haired woman sat smiling at him. She was too thin to be pretty and wore an acid yellow dress that put Cruz in mind of a wasp. He recognized her from the TV.

The reporter. Diane something.

"Hello." He walked over to her. "Call me Cruz."

"Nice to meet you, Cruz. I'm Diane Kinsey." They shook hands.

december wedding

"I know. Have you finished with the interview?" He relaxed his arms at his side, assuming the woman was cataloguing everything about him.

Dusty jeans. Old boots. Hair that needed cutting. Good thing she can't see the titanium plate in my skull, he thought.

"Just about. The crew is doing some lighting work, but I'm done grilling your lady, until tomorrow. I'm sure you're relieved to hear that."

Cruz's neck tightened. "Very relieved."

"I wanted to be the first to tell you that we made some news today. Molly acknowledged that you are her baby daddy. She said she'll confirm it when we film the final interview," Diane said. "So I guess congratulations are in order."

"She did?" All his defenses went up. Molly said she might give the news to the press, but he wondered if the woman was trying to trick him.

"Scout's honor." Diane crossed her heart quickly and then held–up her hand. "You already have a child, don't you? Jesse? Does he live with you and Molly?"

"I'm not answering questions about my son," Cruz said.

"Oh, okay. Sorry." She smiled brightly. "I just asked for background to fill out the story in my mind. I know you never married Jesse's mother, Shar..." she paused. "Did you?"

"No comment."

"Oh, come on, its public record. I could check."

"Be my guest." Cruz narrowed his eyes. "But keep my son out of your story."

"Of course I will. I'm a mother myself, and I understand how you both feel."

Cruz crossed his arms across his massive chest. He knew his size and the scar that ran along the left side of his face were intimidating to people. Sometimes it bothered him.

Today it didn't.

He waited.

Diane took a deep breath. "I was also hoping that Molly would admit that the wedding she's having here next weekend is yours. That would be such fun news for her fans to share!"

Cruz cracked the knuckles on his left hand and stared at the journalist. "We're not getting married next weekend."

"No?" Diane smiled provocatively. "Would you tell me if you were?"

"No."

"Well then, can you tell me who *is* getting married here? *Bake Glory* swears they are delivering a wedding cake next Friday. And Lana Del Ray's people say she is singing at a private engagement in Montecito during Thanksgiving weekend. So someone important is getting married around here."

"No comment."

Diane laughed. "You've got that down, Cruz. Care to wager how many times you've had to say that since Molly divorced Ben Delmonico?"

"Too many." His voice was harsh. Too harsh, Molly would chide. The journalist flinched at his tone and volume.

Cruz cleared his throat, reminding himself that since he'd recovered from the motorcycle accident that had scrambled his brain for a couple of years, the anger he felt at the invasion of his privacy could now be controlled. He just had to slow his thinking down and relax.

Molly could handle these jackals, but so could he as long as he remembered not to get emotional. "It was nice to meet you, Diane. I'd like you to remember, if you can, that Molly tires easily these days, so please don't take advantage of her."

"Oh, I won't. You love her very much, don't you?" Diane took two small steps closer. "It's written all over you. I'm so happy to see that. Molly suffered so much these past couple of years, thanks to that snake she was married to. She deserves to finally have a man like you."

Cruz knew the woman didn't care at all about Molly. She was baiting him. He wasn't going to bite and give her a quote about his feelings for Molly, which she would cheapen by sharing with the world.

"Have a good day." Cruz began to walk away.

"Cruz, is it by any chance Molly's brother who is getting married next Friday?" Diane asked suddenly.

Cruz turned slowly. "What brother?"

"That was just what I was wondering. Molly said she was hosting a family event. But her only brother, Jason, is already married, right? Does Molly have *another* brother?" Diane's green eyes glowed.

Cruz clenched his jaw. "Molly misspoke. She does that when she's tired. It's her friend, Jackson Grant, who is getting married next week. He's an African–American security trader from Chicago and is not related to Molly. And that's confidential information, so please keep it that way, Miss Kinsey, or your on–air interview might get cancelled."

"Well, thank you for your candor, Professor." Diane bit her lip. "And I won't say a thing about Mr. Grant. I promise."

Cruz turned and walked away, careful not to hurry.

Diane watched him with interest until he turned at the end of the house and disappeared. Quickly she grabbed her cell phone from the bench beside her, where it had recorded her exchange with him. She rewound it and hit play, smiling as she heard Cruz's voice.

She punched in a text to her private assistant. "Continue research on Harry Sullivan Jr., New York City. Need birth records and mother's and father's names. Check travel schedule to see if he is coming to CA next week with Jackson Grant, security trader. SULLIVAN IS MHB, I KNOW IT!"

Diane slipped the phone into her purse and hurried out to her car. She already had a headline that Cruz was Molly Harper's baby daddy, which would make the interview soar in the ratings.

With the additional revelation of the secret side to Molly Harper's family tree, she could win an Emmy. *Just in time to negotiate that new contract.*

# # #

"You told her Jackson's *name*?" Molly stared at Cruz as if he was insane, from another planet, or both.

"Yes. I said he was the family friend getting married next Friday. I did that to distract her, because she asked if your brother was getting married."

"My brother!" Molly rested her hand on her throat. "Did she ask about Anne or Harry by name?"

"No. But she did ask if you had *another brother*. Which is why I told her about Jackson, and that he's a close personal friend."

But Jackson is going to marry Harry, who is my half-brother, Molly thought in a panic. *A fact Tonight Magazine researchers will be a whole lot closer to discovering now, thanks to Cruz thinking he was somehow misdirecting Diane Kinsey.* "Oh, God, you shouldn't have said anything, Cruz."

"You shouldn't have said the wedding was a family affair."

"You're right. I shouldn't have." Molly sighed and looked away from him and toward the table full of dirty dinner dishes.

When Marta took Jesse for his bath, Molly had hoped to spend a few quiet minutes with Cruz cleaning up before heading to bed with a book. This news instead injected a huge stressor into what was left of the evening.

Molly picked up some plates. "I didn't confirm there was going to even be a wedding to Diane. She tricked you."

His face flushed. "I told her Jackson's name was confidential."

Molly snorted. "Oh, that'll keep her quiet."

Cruz threw his napkin on the table and started grabbing dishes. "If you hadn't invited that woman into your house in the first place, we wouldn't be talking about this. Especially now. You need to rest, not open our private life more for the press to exploit."

"They weren't in our house. I kept the crew out on the patio. I've done interviews out there before."

december wedding

She knew Cruz was chiding her because he was furious with himself for making the mistake with Diane Kinsey. Molly piled more dishes from her side of the table. She moved too quickly, however, and felt a slight wave of dizziness. She gripped the edge of the table, hoping Cruz didn't notice.

"Sit down." He stared at her intently. "You're pale. Are you feeling okay?"

"I'm fine."

"Please, sit down." He picked up two pieces of silverware. "I'll do the dishes."

"I'll do them. You cooked." She blinked rapidly and tried to clear her head. "I'm not helpless."

"I know that."

"Then stop treating me like I am." Molly slammed another bowl on top of the stack she was precariously building. "I've been making decisions my whole professional life by myself."

He stopped moving. "What are you saying? That you don't need me in your life? You want to be alone? Or that you just don't want to hear it when you do something dumb?"

What am I saying? Her mind was in turmoil. "I'm not telling you I want to be alone. I just wish you would trust my judgment. It was not dumb to do this interview. Stop pushing back on everything I do and accept that I am always going to be an actress. I know how to take care of myself."

He put the dishes down and crossed his arms over his chest. "But you're not just taking care of yourself any more, Molly." His eyes traveled to her stomach. "For the first time in your life, it's not just your life your decisions are impacting. You're worrying yourself sick over how you're going to balance your old life with your new life as a mother. I know this, even if you haven't shared it with me."

"Are you suddenly a mind reader?"

"I'm a Molly-reader. Do you think if you tell me what you're worried about, that I'll press you to give up show business altogether?"

"Wouldn't you?"

He shook his head and looked down. "Aye–yi–yi. How did we get so out of sync, *chica*? I wouldn't ask that of you. But I do think you need to carve out more space for our life. Would it be so bad to let some things go for a while? Like interviews and publicity? Let the other actors in the new movie handle the promotion."

Molly took a deep breath. "I'll think about it."

"Good. And I'll think about keeping my mouth shut, no matter what anyone asks me about next week's wedding."

She widened her eyes. "Thanks." Molly set the dishes down wearily and wiped her hands on a napkin. "I better call Jackson and warn him Kinsey's people will be calling."

"I already called and told Harry," Cruz said. "He said we shouldn't worry about it. He also said to tell you he agrees, no press in the house." Cruz grinned. "He told me the first time you invited him here, he looked in the medicine cabinet. So, there's no telling *where* they looked."

Cruz chuckled, hoping her brother's humor would diffuse the tension whirling around them.

Molly bit her lip and headed for the house. "No headlines there. All they'd find is prenatal vitamins and suntan lotion."

He reached out and stopped her in her tracks. "Leave the kitchen. Go to the den and put your feet up. We've got a full week coming, and you need to rest."

They both looked down at her bare legs. Her ankles were red and swollen from fluid retention. "They look bad tonight. My feet are wide as snowshoes. I'll never wear high heels again."

Cruz drew her into his arms. "I like a woman who doesn't tip over easily." He kissed the top of her head. "Will you marry me?"

She started to say a curt 'no', but when she looked into his eyes, there was something new there she had never seen before. He was not asking lightly, being impatient, or trying to exert his will.

And he wasn't expressing a macho wish to tie her to him more closely so he could somehow protect her, something she would felt behind his words in the past.

No, tonight's proposal was different. She caught a glimmer of vulnerability in the big, tough guy embracing her. *Did he long to belong to her, and not want things the other way around.* "Is it so important to you? To get married now?" she asked.

"Yes."

"Is it because of the baby?" Cruz was Catholic and so traditional, she thought. She put her hand on his cheek. "You know we'll always share equally in every decision governing our child's life."

"I know that. But I don't want to marry you because we're having a child." Cruz held her shoulders so tenderly she hardly felt his hands. "I want to marry you because of you. Because of me. We belong together, and we always have. I know you're not a big believer in convention, but you believe in love. You have shown me that since I met you and even more these past couple of years. You saved my life. Which is why I want to formally, under all the laws created by man and God, pledge myself to you forever. To claim you. To thank you. *Mi familia.*"

Tears flooded down her cheeks. "Yes. I will marry you, Cruz Morales."

She saw immediately that though he had spoken from the heart, he had not expected this answer. He had bared his soul to her, but her words stunned him.

Cruz folded her into an embrace, lifted her off the ground, and danced them around in a circle. They were both breathless and laughing when he finally sat her down.

"When?" he said. "Now that you've agreed, I feel I better get a commitment."

"I don't know." Molly laughed. "This Spring? Or June, maybe? After the baby, okay? We don't really have time to plan anything before then."

"How about tomorrow? At the courthouse in Santa Barbara."

"No, no, no. If we're going to do this, we need to do this right. Your mother will want to be there. And we want dear Jesse with us, and we can't just spring this on him. Please, Cruz, we can wait a few months."

"We can." He grinned. "You've made me so happy, Molly." He kissed the side of her face. "Now go get comfortable in the den. I'll bring Jesse in for story time. He loves when you read to him."

"Okay. But let's keep this between us, until after Harry gets married. I don't want to distract anyone from his big day."

"Of course." His eyes shined. "It'll be our secret. Now, go sit. I'll do the dishes."

Molly nodded and wearily headed to her favorite area of the house. *What have I done?* she thought suddenly, but not with regret. She was filled with wonder and happiness. She had not realized until she had agreed to marry Cruz, just how much she wanted that connection, too.

Molly collapsed on the leather sectional in the den and turned on the light beside her. There was a pile of children's books on the table, old ones of hers and Jason's; along with several new ones she had bought for Jesse.

He was almost four now, speaking more and more about everything. He loved books. Especially those about *Lowly Worm*, and anything with birds. He was a sweet child. Fair like his mother, Shar, and blessed with Cruz's serious dark eyes and lush lashes.

Cruz and Shar shared custody of Jesse, but they had had him full–time for the last month and would until just before the baby was due, when Shar returned from a temporary job in Europe.

Molly felt closer to the toddler now than she had in the past, although she did fret over how he would feel when the new baby arrived. Now that they were going to be married,

december wedding

she would have to try extra hard to make sure Jesse felt secure and equal in the new family unit.

She knew from experience how easy it was to wound a child by sending the wrong message about their importance to the family. When Molly discovered at age five that her parents were hiding the truth of her adoption, her young mind equated their secret keeping with shame, and she was convinced something was wrong with adoption, *and with her*, or her parents would not have hidden the fact.

It was not until she was older and discussed it with Norma that she understood they had concealed the truth out of a misplaced worry that she would not feel as loved if she knew the truth.

Molly blinked. *No secrets. That's going to be my philosophy when talking about things with my child*, she promised herself. *I am sure to make mistakes, but not that one.*

"Here's Jesse, all clean and ready for story time," Marta announced from the doorway. Cruz's silver-haired mother, carrying the scrubbed up little bundle in his pj's, beamed the contented smile she had had on her face since the day Jesse was born. "He wants to read about Lowly Worm."

"Do you want to hear about Lowly, Jesse?" Molly asked.

"And the talking bread," he said, referring to his favorite story about a baby doll who gets accidently baked into a baguette.

Marta set her grandson down, and he scampered up onto the sofa and into Molly's arms. He nestled against her side while his small left hand patted her on the stomach.

"Hello, baby," he said, mimicking Cruz's voice and mannerisms.

Molly kissed his damp curls. "Are you looking forward to being a big brother, Jesse?"

He nodded. "Molly, can baby sleep with me?"

"In your big boy bed?"

"Yes. In my room."

"Well, sure. Sometimes. But I might have to sleep with you too, and make sure baby doesn't fall out."

"I won't let the baby fall," Jesse said seriously.

"Oh, of course you wouldn't." Molly gave him a hug. "Baby is lucky to have you for a brother, Jesse."

The little boy grinned then suddenly turned his head and kissed Molly's belly. "I love you baby! Can you hear me?"

His spontaneous show of affection brought tears to both women's eyes.

"I'm going to go put some laundry on. You two rest. You want tea?" Marta asked.

"Please."

"I want Lowly and the talking bread!" Jesse pointed to the book.

Marta wiped her hand across her eyes and then went to get the tea. Molly put aside the book about welcoming a newborn and reached instead for Jesse's requested story. His sunny happiness tonight made her feel a lot less worried about how he was going to take the coming changes.

I should be more like Jesse, she thought. With a lighter heart than she'd had for months, Molly picked up the Richard Scary book and began to read.

chapter three

Taping the final interview with *Tonight Magazine* went well, better actually, than Molly had expected. Diane Kinsey did not refer to any possible half-brothers Molly might be hiding.

While she did not kid herself that the newswoman was not digging around trying to find a story, she decided Kinsey had enough good sense to concentrate on the scoop she had.

Diane *had* brought up Norma's death the year before, asking her if she and her mother had always been close. She followed with a comment about Molly's well-known quest for keeping her private life out of the public eye, but didn't rehash Cruz's accident or her failed marriage to Ben Delmonico.

At the end of the taping, Molly wished Diane good luck and walked with her to the front door, waving as the journalist, along with Artie Stein, drove off. As she went past the kitchen, she was tempted to grab one of the sweet rolls or sandwiches sitting on the counter because she hadn't eaten for hours, but she had to pee first.

Molly hurried into her bedroom, leaving Celia out on the patio to handle the breakdown of the set by the camera crew. She stripped off her clothes, feeling confident in what she'd chosen for the interview. The gauzy pink mini-dress flattered her coloring, while the leather flats hid her snowshoe feet.

She chuckled about Cruz's comments last night. He was right. As wide as her feet were now, there was little chance of her tipping over. At the sink, she rubbed off her makeup, which was industrial level and more effective today, and turned on the shower.

A moment later, she stepped in.

The fog of steam hit her in the face, and she immediately felt dizzy. Molly grabbed the bar on the glass door and steadied herself, thinking it must be the heat getting to her, but when she blinked, the floor seemed to tilt.

I can't fall. The baby... She clutched at her belly with her other arm as her knees began to buckle.

Someone knocked on the closed bathroom door. "Molly, Senora Sullivan is here. Do you want her to wait for you?"

Marta.

Molly gulped and filled her lungs as the room began a slow spin. She bent her knees and let herself collapse onto the tile floor inside the shower. The water ran hot and steady, hitting her on the face when she turned toward the bathroom door.

Panic exploded inside of her as she remembered she had locked the door because the news crew was outside.

"Marta! Get Cruz and tell him the door is locked. Hurry, please. I'm very sick!" She clutched her belly, pleading with God not to let her die. A moment later, the world went black.

# # #

Molly's consciousness returned, and the first thing she heard was Cruz yelling at the 9-1-1 operator. Jesse was crying somewhere in the background. Other voices, nervous and urgent, mingled with the boy's.

Anne Sullivan's face loomed into view. "Molly, can you speak?" Anne took Molly's hand and pressed two fingers to Molly's wrist. "Can you hear me?"

"Yes." Molly blinked. She was lying on her bed, a blanket on top of her.

"Did you faint? Hit your head in the shower?" Anne's voice was calm as she glanced down at her wristwatch.

"No. No, I didn't fall. I felt dizzy, and then I couldn't seem to stand, and then I was nauseous." She trembled. "I was so scared. Is the baby okay?"

december wedding

"Don't get ahead of yourself, Molly. I think everything's fine," Anne said.

"Jesus H. Christ, Molly." Cruz suddenly appeared on the other side of the bed, his eyes wild. "What happened? Did you hit your head?"

"Cruz, step back for a moment and let Molly catch her breath." Anne's voice was firm.

Taking a step backwards, Cruz watched Anne like a hawk as the former nurse placed a cool cloth on Molly's forehead. "She said she didn't hit her head, Cruz. She felt dizzy and blacked out."

"I'm sure I didn't fall on my belly. So the baby should be okay, right?" Molly's voice rose and she tried to sit-up.

Anne gently pressed a hand against Molly's shoulder. "Babies are very well padded and protected inside of mom, so just calm down and let me make sure you're okay." She peered closely at Molly's eyes. "You are sure you didn't fall?"

Molly blew out a breath and rubbed her forehead. "I didn't, I sort of sank down on my knees, and then onto my butt because I was dizzy. But I'm sure I didn't hit my head or anything." She folded both hands over her stomach. "I did pass out, though. Do you think I hurt the baby?"

Anne patted Molly's hands. "No. I don't think you hurt the baby or yourself at all. You don't have any wounds or marks on you that I saw when Cruz carried you in here. And while your pulse is a little fast, its fine and your pupils are normal. When the EMTs get here, they'll take your blood pressure, and we'll know more what to do next."

"She's going to the hospital." Cruz ran his hand through his hair. "Are you still dizzy, *chica?* What did you eat today?"

"I, ah, I had oatmeal this morning. No, I'm not dizzy." She looked from Cruz to Anne. "Can I sit up now?"

"Yes, but let me help you." She grasped Molly's hand and the actress sat upright and glanced around the room. Marta waited at the doorway, her eyes huge.

"Don't worry, Marta. Where's Jesse?" Molly asked.

"He's with Aunt Rosa," Cruz said. He sat carefully next to Molly on the bed and squeezed her shoulder. "You're going to the hospital."

"Stop saying that, okay? I don't think I need to." She glanced toward the hallway. "Where is the film crew? Did they leave?"

"They're in the front yard, loading up their trucks," Marta said.

"Thank God for that." Molly looked at Cruz. "Why don't you go open the gate for them and make sure they're off the property before the EMTs get here?"

"You should not have let them inside the house," Cruz said. "We're never having an interview here again."

"Cruz, their being here isn't what made me dizzy."

"Yes it is. You didn't eat properly or rest for the last six hours because of them." His voice rose and he stood. "I'll make sure they leave now."

As if on cue, the sound of an ambulance siren drifted in the window, getting louder by the second.

"Jackals," Cruz muttered as he headed to the hallway.

"Don't make a scene, Cruz. Please," Molly pleaded.

He stopped. "Don't worry, I won't." Cruz looked at Anne. "Stay with her please, until I get back."

"I won't leave her, Cruz."

"Thank you." He left, and Marta hurried after him.

Molly folded her arms over her chest. "Well, this will be a big test of how well he can control his anger issues."

"He's much improved since last year, in my opinion. The medication must be working well," Anne said.

"Yes. And also the therapy. He has a handle on it, and most of his memory has fully returned. He's very much the same guy I first fell in love with."

"Good. And I don't blame him for being worried. Like most men, he is taking his frustration and fear out on others right now. But once he sees you're fine, he'll calm down."

"Do you think I'm really okay?"

"Yes. Yes I do," Anne said. "But you should go to the hospital and get checked out. The baby is due in what, just six weeks?"

"Seven," Molly answered. "That could get crazy. You know the press will show up if I am there. Word always gets out"

"Why don't we call your OBGYN and arrange to go to her office? If the EMTs say you are fine, I'll drive you to the doctor, and she can check you out. You can duck down in the back seat, just in case the news people are hanging around on the street."

"That's a good idea. Thank you." Molly rubbed her hands up and down her arms. "Jeez, now I've got goose bumps. Do you think my not eating, along with the heat from the steam in the shower caused the dizziness?"

"Did you keep hydrated today?"

"No. I didn't want to have to stop and go to the bathroom ten times."

"Well, that's probably what caused you to faint." Anne patted Molly's hand. "You told me when we talked last week that your doctor said everything was fine. Blood pressure and urine tests, right? As soon as the EMTs say you're okay, I'll get you a drink of orange juice. It'll help if it was low blood sugar."

Suddenly Molly began to tear–up. "I feel like an idiot. How am I going to take care of a little baby if I can't even take care of myself?"

Anne drew back, surprised. "Oh, Molly, you're going to do great."

"I don't know about that. Hell, I can't even remember something simple like drink water every hour. This is going to be a disaster. Maybe I should hire a nanny. Cruz doesn't want me to, and I didn't want to, but..."

"Molly, don't be too hard on yourself. As you know, pregnant women have all their normal fears amplified by hormones. You're going to learn as you go, and it will all be fine. After all, you just helped produce a multi–million dollar movie, right? You will be able to handle a little baby. Besides, Cruz will be with you. And Marta. You've got family."

Including me, Anne said with her eyes.

Molly sighed. She had been hard on Anne, the woman who had given birth to her, when she came into her life eighteen months ago. Since then they had become friends, and Molly was so grateful that Anne never seemed to feel awkward around her. She was like Norma in that way.

I can trust her, too, Molly realized.

The actress reached for Anne's hand. "It might sound crazy, but since I've been pregnant, I've been more anxious and nervous that ever before in my life. I lay awake at night, worried sick."

"What are you worried about, Molly?"

"Change. My entire life is going to change by becoming a mother. And Cruz and I are getting married." She slapped her hand over her mouth. "Oh my God, that's top secret. Please don't say anything."

"I won't." Anne leaned closer. "But how exciting."

"It feels like we can both handle it now, even though I still doubt Cruz can ever learn to take the media intrusions in stride." She shook her head. "My bigger worry is that I don't know how I'm going to ever go back to work with a baby. We've had Jesse full time the past few weeks, and it's staggering how I don't have time to do anything but watch him. With the new baby, it'll be even worse." Her voice broke.

"You take it one day at a time, like everyone else." Anne's expression was wistful. "My advice is to give yourself time without trying to be perfect at everything."

"That's good advice, Anne. But I worry so much about Cruz, and now about the baby, who is also going to have to deal with publicity from the moment it's born." She looked at Anne squarely. "Speaking of publicity, I need to warn you, a journalist may be on to the fact that Harry is my half-brother. Which means you might get outed as my birth mother."

Anne leaned forward. "Who would be interested in that?"

"No one, really. However, it'll be *news* because I have never announced it. Then it can be *revealed* by the press, which is just what I was saying. It's always a battle to keep my personal life private. I've tried to keep some things just for me my entire working life, and now my baby's going to grow up and have to learn it can't say certain things to certain people." Molly rubbed her eyes. "I hate giving the poor kid that baggage."

Before Anne could reply, Cruz rushed back into the room, trailed by Celia.

"The EMTs are here. The film crew drove off the property, but stopped in the street and asked what was going on. I told them the gardener was sick."

"Fast thinking," Anne said.

So much for Cruz learning to say nothing, Molly thought. "Okay. I need to get up and put something on as I'm naked under the blankets."

"I'll help you." Celia pushed past Cruz. "Why don't we all give Molly some privacy?" She grabbed a loose fitting nightgown and a robe off the chair by the bed, handed it to her, and then herded everyone out the door.

Everyone but Cruz, who looked like he would bite anyone who tried to make him leave.

Molly slipped on her gown and some panties, pulled the robe closed and ran her hand through her damp hair. She glanced at the image in the dresser mirror and saw a pale, heavily pregnant woman who looked as if she had been stranded in the rain forest for days.

The sounds of men talking and equipment rolling across the Spanish tile floors got closer. She quickly slipped on her pink flats and buttoned the robe. "Cruz, did you tell them on the phone who I was?"

"Yes." He put his arm around her gently. "It was one time I thought I should, so they'd get here faster."

"Well, that's good news." She grinned weakly. "Because if you hadn't told them they were coming to see Molly Harper, I'm sure no one would recognize me."

chapter four

"So you're sure she and the baby are fine now?" Harry Jr. turned to his mother. "You wouldn't keep it from me if there was something to worry about, would you?"

"No, of course not." Anne turned the water on in the sink to cover the huge pan full of potatoes she had just peeled for tomorrow's dinner.

"The baby's due January 19. Two days before my birthday. Maybe it will be late," Harry said.

"Don't wish that on your sister." Anne lifted the heavy pan onto the stove and then glanced out the window to the back yard. John Wright was out in his garden, harvesting the last of the vegetables for the feast tomorrow.

She and John were cooking Thanksgiving dinner for her sons and their families, as well as Molly, Cruz, and his mother and son. Excitement and worry knotted together in her stomach. It would be the first time she had hosted all three of her children at a holiday dinner. Something she thought she would never do.

"I love your hair, by the way, Mom. It looks great with those blonde highlights. Brings out your blue eyes."

"Why, thank you." Anne glanced at Harry, who was sitting in her kitchen in Santa Barbara, chopping onions and celery for the turkey dressing. He and Jackson, his fiancé, had flown in from New York last night for Thanksgiving, to be followed by their wedding at Molly's the next day.

"You're welcome. Since you and John got together, you've looked ten years younger."

"He doesn't like hairspray." Anne brushed her hands on the apron she wore over her sweater and jeans. "And he likes jeans. Your dad did too, but I always thought once I was bigger than a size 12 and older than fifty, that jeans were out."

Harry gave her an appraising look. "It's not the size, it's the attitude." He raised his eyebrows. "You're fifty–two and you've still got it going on, lady." Harry turned back to his work. "When are my big brother, Maria, and the rug rat getting in?"

"Eric said they'd leave about ten tomorrow morning. What time are Jackson's parents arriving?" Anne glanced at the clock. "Too bad you two groups couldn't have flown in at the same time. I hate that you have to go back to LAX tomorrow night."

"No sweat, *madre bonita*." Harry grinned. "Cruz says that means pretty mother." He carried the chopping board over to the stove and scraped his veggies into the sauté pan. "Jackson's parents already had scheduled Thanksgiving plans with Mrs. Grant's family, so they're taking a seven o'clock plane from San Francisco. We'll pick them up and have everyone back to the hotel by nine. What time is our turkey dinner tomorrow?"

"Three p.m. I thought that would give everyone time to relax a little after the wedding rehearsal at noon."

"Seems kind of dumb to have a rehearsal." Harry dropped a scoop of butter into the pan. "I mean, there's going to be thirty of us. Jackson, Reverend Helen, and I will stand at the fountain in the middle of Molly's patio. No one is giving either of us away. What's to practice?"

"It's always good to do a run–through." Anne fanned herself. Her menopausal symptoms were less lethal than a year ago, but cooking always made her hormones go into overdrive. She read somewhere that the sense of smell during the transition from fertile to unfertile, sharpened, and she thought that was true. She could smell the flowers in the garden even when the door was closed.

"Hot?" Harry waved a towel at his mother.

"Not bad." She smiled at her youngest child. He reminded her more and more of his father, who had died four years ago at a much too young sixty-four. "Your dad would have so loved to see you happily married."

"You think so?" Harry's tone was skeptical. "He was great when I told him I was gay, but I wonder what he'd think about Jackson and me getting formally married."

"He would have been supportive, and delighted that you'd found the right person to spend your life with."

Harry beamed. "Jackson's Dad is cool with it too, but I have doubts about Lily."

"Jackson's mother is against you two marrying?"

"I wouldn't go that far. But you can tell she's uncomfortable about it." He raised his eyebrows, a twinkle shining in his eyes. "I think she's hung up on what to say to her friends. Some of her church ladies consider us sinners."

"She needs to remind her friends that we're all sinners. Now watch what you're doing and don't burn the onions." Anne swatted him playfully and walked out to the backyard.

"How's it going over there? You want a beer?" she called out to John.

"Hey, gorgeous." John walked to the fence and met Anne, leaning over to give her a kiss. "Don't touch me. I'm all sweaty."

She perused his tall, rangy form. His dark hair was balding, and his muscled, tan arms were not those of a young man, but to her John Wright at sixty was gorgeous. "I've kissed you when you were sweaty."

"I remember. Last night, right? Thank you for that, by the way. I like it when you're on top."

"You're welcome. Now stop talking about sex. Harry's right inside."

"I think Harry's had sex." John raised his eyebrows.

"Very funny." She sighed. "Gosh, I'm so nervous about dinner tomorrow. What is it about entertaining that makes me feel inadequate?"

"I don't know. I think you're too hard on yourself. You will end up enjoying it, you know. Especially since everyone coming is family. Except for me."

"You're family," she said.

"Not officially, but you do make me feel welcome." He handed Anne a basket of veggies over the fence. "Here you go. How about you? You going to enjoy the day when your youngest gets hitched?"

"Yes." Tears stung, but she blinked them away. "I'm feeling raw over the fact Harry and Eric's dad isn't alive to see this. But yes, it's going to be great."

"He'll be there with all of you," John said. "In here." He tapped his chest. "He must have been quite a man to have helped raise those two boys of yours. They're terrific."

"Thanks, John."

"For what?"

Anne kissed his cheek. "For understanding me so well and for not blowing it off when I'm worried. Cruz reminds me of you in that way. He senses when Molly is fretting and lets her talk about it. It's a good thing."

"I'm glad they ended up together. Has she said any more about journalists poking around, trying to find out about you being her mother?"

"No. Just that comment last week, the day she fainted in the shower. I talked to her yesterday on the phone, but she didn't mention anything else."

"Well, let's hope the paparazzi stay scarce and go to their own Thanksgiving dinner get–togethers."

"You don't think they'd just show up here, do you?"

"I doubt it. I'll turn the hose on them if they do."

Anne laughed and pushed her hair off her forehead. It always fell in her eyes since she stopped using hair spray, but she liked the way it felt. "Harry's a little worried about Jackson's mom. He thinks she's not totally supportive of gays marrying."

"Oh." John shrugged. "She's not alone there, Anne. Lots of folks look at gays being in love as something other than humans being in love, but I am sure she will keep her opinions to herself. If not, well, she's coming to the wrong place this weekend."

"Jackson is her only child and her father is a Baptist minister, so she probably just has to work harder at accepting new things on that front. But she's thrilled about meeting Molly from what I understand."

"Did Jackson tell his folks Molly is Harry's half-sister?"

"No. Molly gave Harry her blessing to tell any family member he wanted to, but Jackson opted to keep it quiet. The fewer people know about it, the better, he said. I tend to agree." Anne bit her lip. "It's amazing how me giving her up for adoption when I was a sixteen year-old girl still has ramifications to her happiness today."

"That's true with everything, isn't it?" John squeezed her arm. "You did the generous thing back then, as Molly has even said. It is her choice to keep the fact she was adopted quiet if she wants. If it comes out, it comes out. It won't be your fault."

"I know, but I still worry. Last thing she needs now is more stress."

"The last thing you need to do is worry over things you can't change, Mrs. Sullivan."

"Good advice, Mr. Wright."

They kissed quickly but meaningfully and then Anne walked back to the house. "Stop staring at my rear end," she called over her shoulder.

John grinned. "Never."

chapter five

Molly pushed away from the table. "I honestly feel like I'm going to explode," she said. "And it has nothing to do with being eight months pregnant."

Anne's guests all nodded and smiled in agreement.

"A toast to the hostess with the mostess." Harry Jr. raised his wine glass. "Fabulous job, Mother. Your three children and their significant others are very impressed. And your turkey ain't bad either."

"Your gravy is to die for," Jackson chimed in.

"To the hostess," many voices seconded, including three-year old Jesse and Anne's grandson, Andrew, who bumped their juice boxes together and giggled.

"Thank you all for coming." Anne blew a kiss toward John, who sat at the other side of the table, and then to Harry. "And to all of you for your help and delicious side dishes. Jackson, I've never had better cranberry orange relish in my life."

"It's a secret recipe," the handsome, soon to be married, Jackson teased. "It has sugar and a dollop of orange liquor."

"And I've got a shot or two of *cointreau* in me too," Harry joked.

"You've got a shot or two of other things in you as well, Harry Sullivan Jr." Anne's elder son, Eric, stood as the comments degenerated into banter. "Here's to my brother, who doesn't deserve Jackson, and to Jackson, I wish you good luck. You're going to need it."

"To Harry and Jackson," the guests said in unison.

"I'm going to wash the young men up and take them into the other room," Maria, Eric's wife, said.

december wedding

Marta and the others began to clear the table.

"Molly, why don't you go turn on the football game for the men and put your feet up. We'll take care of the dishes," Anne said.

"Grand idea, Anne." Cruz smiled as he took the plates from Molly and motioned with his chin. "I'll bring you some tea."

"Thank you," she said.

Molly stopped in the bathroom for the tenth time that day and then walked into Anne's comfortable living room, full of sofas, chairs, and good lighting. She glanced appreciatively at the original floral prints of local California plants, which Anne avidly collected.

The front door was open, and a breeze wafted in through the screen. Molly shivered but enjoyed the change of temperature as December approached. She walked around the room, touching the photographs and pottery pieces Anne collected. There was a small framed photo of her, Harry, and Eric, discreetly set with several others.

There aren't any of me and Anne, Molly thought. *I'll have Cruz take one tonight. Anne would never ask, but I'm sure she would like one.*

She heard Maria and the little boys in the bedroom behind her, and John, Jackson, and Eric Sullivan out in the backyard. They were throwing the football around.

Molly sat on the window seat, propping herself against the cushions. She put her legs up and rested her hands on her stomach, which seemed to be growing noticeably by the day. She closed her eyes.

In a few weeks, her baby would be here. She would be harried and more sleep-deprived than she was now, but a thrill ran through her bones at the thought of holding her own child. Neither she nor Cruz had looked at the sonogram screen when the technician asked if they wanted to know the sex.

They wanted it to be a surprise, though Cruz was sure it was a boy. "Name him for the man who raised you," Cruz had suggested. "Norma would have loved another Charles in the world."

Molly said that they should wait until they met the child to pick a name, mostly because she felt in her heart that the baby was a girl.

Her grandmother, Norma's mother, was named Emma. Molly tried that on in her head many times. Maybe she and Cruz could give Jesse a choice of two or three names and let him choose, she thought. *Would he like that? I will have to be sure not to let Lowly Worm be one of the choices.*

"Hey, gorgeous." Harry walked up next to her.

Molly opened her eyes and smiled. "Hey, yourself."

He handed her a cup of tea on a saucer. "Your old man told me to bring you this. He's washing the turkey pan and ingratiating himself further with our mother."

Harry was the only one in the Sullivan family who freely referred to their blood ties since he first found out she was his half-sister. It had unsettled her a year ago, but now she was touched when he did. She and Harry had an immediate affinity of spirit, and she loved him as she did Jason, the brother she was raised with.

"Anne's nobody's fool. She recognizes a good man when she has one willing to deal with dirty dishes." Molly smiled. "Those are hard to find."

"I think she's in love with John Wright."

"I agree. How do you feel about that?"

Harry grinned. "I just want the woman to be happy." He moved her legs over and sat beside her on the window seat. "So, how you feeling? Not too tired to have all of us trekking back to your place tomorrow?"

"No. I'm looking forward to Jackson making an honest man out of you. Besides, I won't be doing anything. Your caterer made it clear I was to stay out of my kitchen until he and his people cleared out after the ceremony."

"Good for him." He patted her stomach. "How's the baby?"

"Good. Good."

"Mom told me about you fainting last week. What was that all about?"

"All my fault. Wasn't eating and drinking right."

"I'm glad you're okay."

"Me too," she said. "I'm thrilled you chose Reverend Helen to do your wedding service, by the way. Cruz has known her for years because of a program they did with her school and the university. I've not known her long, but she is one of those people you like right off. What she's doing to help immigrant children is amazing."

"She is. They have provided education and housing for a couple of thousand children over the last two years. She is making a difference. Just the kind of church lady I like."

"One of her schools is near my place in Taos. You and I will have to go see her if you guys ever come visit."

"I'd love that. Maybe she can put your picture on her fundraising mailing." He grinned. "I know you hate mixing your personal friends with business, but you might make her some moola for the kids."

They both laughed at that, well aware of the truth of it. . Chimes sounded from the clock above the fireplace. "When are you and Jackson going to the airport?" Molly asked.

"Right now." Jackson said as he walked into the room. Tall and bronze, with flashing dark eyes, the securities trader looked more like a movie star than most of the actors Molly knew. An opinion that tickled Harry when she'd told him that.

"You ready, Harry? You know you can stay and chat up Molly if you want to. I can drive myself."

"Yeah, and get lost despite the GPS? Four times between here and Ventura, like when we arrived? No sir. You're not ducking out on me that easily."

Jackson grinned. Harry kissed Molly on the cheek and patted her belly. "Okay. See you tomorrow, Miss Molly."

"Thank you again for letting us get married at your place," Jackson said. "It's perfect. Private and beautiful."

"Well, we'll hope it stays private," she said.

"It will," Harry said.

"Guys, did you get any weird calls this week from anyone trying to find out if you were related to me?"

The men exchanged a quick look. "Well, actually, Jackson's secretary fielded a call from a guy who said he was calling from *The Daily Post*. He wanted to know if he knew you. She blew him off," Harry said.

"They mentioned my name?" She did not like the sound of that.

"Yeah. But Chloe said she never heard of you and hung up." Jackson smiled. "Of course she loves your movies, but she's sharp enough to shut down a fishing–expedition by a news person. She knows about the wedding, but she's the only one who does at my firm."

"I like how Chloe thinks." Molly swung her feet onto the floor. "Let me walk you outside. I could use a little exercise to help me digest the four helpings of desserts I just ate."

The trio headed out the door to the crowded driveway, while Harry and Jackson bickered over who was driving the rental. Molly took a deep breath and rubbed her arms. She needed a sweater tonight. Fall in California was chilly most evenings, even though the blue skies and sunshine continued during the day.

She waved as Harry backed out and drove down the street. A flash of light near the trees across the street caught her eye. After a moment, she spotted the source. Two houses down from Anne's, a man in a baseball cap held a camera with a huge lens, pointed directly at her.

"Molly?"

She turned abruptly at the sound of Cruz's voice. He was watching her from the porch, smiling. "Do you need a sweater? We can go for a walk if you want some exercise."

"No. No, let's just help with the cleanup and go home. I'm bushed."

Cruz must have heard something in her voice. He cocked his head to the side and scanned the street behind her. "Son of a bitch." He bit the last word off angrily as he walked down the steps.

She grabbed his arm. "Leave it. Don't give the idiot any photos he can use. Just come inside with me."

Cruz glared at her for a moment, but immediately calmed down. He threw his arm around her shoulders and they walked back into Anne's house without another glance.

Everyone was outside in the backyard with the football, except for the little boys who sat on the sofa, Ninja turtles in hand. Marta was with them.

"We're almost ready to go, Mom." Cruz stopped and gave Jesse a kiss. "We're just going out to say goodbye."

"Okay."

"I don't want to go, Daddy," Jesse complained.

"Okay, five more minutes, *mejo*."

Molly smiled and followed Cruz outside to see everyone off.

"Dinner was delicious, Anne. Thank you so much for hosting all of us," Molly said, as the women headed back into the house.

"My pleasure. Let me come in with you. I've got leftovers for sandwiches if anyone wants one later tonight."

"You know me pretty well."

"I remember you like onions and cranberry sauce on your sandwiches," Anne replied. "I put a couple in for Jason, too. Is he coming tomorrow morning?"

"Yes. He and his wife are driving down. He had to have dinner with her folks today, but I know he'd rather have been here with us."

"Your brother's a doll." She turned to Cruz. "There's also some pumpkin pie. It's all in the bag on the counter."

They went back into the kitchen and Cruz took the bag and thanked Anne warmly for her hospitality. As they were leaving, Anne's old-fashioned wall phone rang. "Goodbye, you two. I'll see you in the morning," she said, before turning to answer the call.

Twenty minutes later Molly, Cruz, and the family were back at the house in Montecito. When they left Anne's, Molly was relieved to see that the guy with the camera wasn't outside, and there was no sign of him at her house.

Marta busied herself putting Jesse to bed and said an early good night as Molly and Cruz settled into the den.

The actress yawned and leaned her head against his shoulder.

"You want to watch a movie, *chica*? We can watch one with my favorite actress. An old one of yours is on TCM tonight." He turned on the television.

"No, thanks, you know I hate to watch myself. I am just going to sit here and fall asleep in five minutes. And maybe get up in an hour and have a turkey sandwich."

He grinned. "Sounds like a good plan."

Molly snuggled next to him and heard her phone ringing in her purse. She had left it on the table in the kitchen.

"I'll get it," Cruz said.

"No. Leave it. No one needs to tell me anything on Thanksgiving night that can't wait until tomorrow. I'm just going to sit here and count my blessings."

Cruz kissed her and flipped channels to one of the ever-present football games. Then his phone, which never rang, sang out. He slipped it out of the pocket of his jeans and looked down. "It's Anne."

Molly's heart jerked a little. She reached for the phone. "Hello? Anne, its Molly." She listened for several seconds and then gasped. "Oh no. How terrible. I'm so sorry."

"What's wrong?" Cruz demanded.

"Jackson's father had a heart attack at the airport in San Francisco," Molly said. "Harry just called her and told her to cancel the wedding."

# # #

Diane Kinsey sat at the conference table in her office and looked through the stack of photos her staff had assembled.

Phil Curran, her producer, hung up his phone and sighed. "Molly had the caterer take all the food to the Santa

december wedding

Barbara Mission food kitchen. The cake too. No one from the mission will confirm it, but the driver who delivered it there is sending us some photos."

"For how much?"

"Five hundred."

Diane frowned. "How's Grant's father?"

"Pretty bad, I guess. They did a triple bypass, but he's going to be in intensive care for a week at least, according to the nurse I talked to."

"You got a *nurse* to talk to you?"

"I'm persuasive."

"How much?"

"Seven hundred and fifty."

"Is Harry Sullivan still in Frisco with the Grant family?"

"We don't know."

Diane scrunched up her face. "How's that possible? Is he wearing his cloak of invisibility like Harry Potter?"

"The hotel porter hasn't seen him, Diane. I have people at his New York apartment, but no one there has seen him either. I say you just call his cell and ask him on the record if he's Molly's brother."

She sat back in her chair and crossed her toned arms over her smart Chanel dress. "No. I am not going to do that. I think we need to play this carefully. Molly can still pull the plug on the interview, or try to, and her guys are really good at casting her as the victim."

"But it's already December first. You have twenty days before you have to give her the final tape and twenty-five days before we air. I say we hold the adoption story until after the holidays. You've already got great stuff in the interview with her naming Cruz as her baby-daddy."

Diane stared out the window. "I want more than that." She took a deep breath. "Let's put the cancelled wedding story out there, but give it a little twist."

"Meaning what?"

"Do you still have those ass hats at *The Daily Post* in your pocket?"

Phil grimaced. "We use each other from time to time. It'll cost me a dinner, though. If not cold hard cash."

"Call them." She pushed a stack of photos over to him of Molly and Cruz taken over the last couple of months. The top one was of Molly at *Saks* being fitted for a dress. "I'm sure they'll be interested in hearing about poor Molly Harper being left at the altar the day after Thanksgiving."

"What?" Phil was shocked. "I can't tell *The Daily Post* it was Molly's wedding that got cancelled. We know it was Harry Sullivan and Jackson Grant who were getting married."

"We do?" Diane shook her head. "I don't know that. I never got confirmation of that from Molly. She never said there was a wedding going on at all. Cruz did. But of course, he was on orders to lie. Unless you heard something I didn't?"

Phil shook his head. "But why do that? People like her. They are going to be upset if they think she was dumped again. I mean, the Ben Delmonico story was tough enough for her and her fans to live through."

"You getting soft on me, Phil?"

He cleared his throat, hearing the threat. "No. But what's the angle?"

"A story like this will whet the public's appetite to find out what really happened to Molly. I bet she will even give me an updated sit–down, just to knock the *Post's* story all to hell. She might even cough–up her real wedding date!"

"Seems dangerous, Diane. *Tonight Magazine* has a good reputation. If Molly finds out we are behind the rumor being pushed by the tabloids, they will go to the brass. It won't be pretty."

"What rumor?" Diane stood up and smoothed some non–existent wrinkles from her skirt. "I've got lunch with a Fox VP. Going to get the skinny on who is being cancelled. See you later, Phil." She cut her eyes to the prints. "And be sure and send the sleazebags a couple of photos that show just

december wedding

how pregnant Molly is, okay? Her ankles were huge during the interview. Poor thing."

chapter six

Molly, Celia, Harry, Anne, and Reverend Helen Nunez sat down to have lunch and discuss how and where to reschedule Harry and Jackson's wedding.

"Jackson's adamant we do it before the end of the year," Harry said. "His father is pushing him because Mr. Grant thinks he's going to die. It's not very romantic, but Jackson's trying to humor the guy."

"How is Mr. Grant?" Molly asked. "And will he be able to attend if you have it anywhere but his hospital room?"

"He's being released today, actually," Harry said. "Jackson's gone back to San Francisco, and they're all flying home to Los Alamos this afternoon. Jackson said his dad is doing remarkably well, except for this obsession that he's not going to live much longer."

"Depression is a common side effect of having a heart attack," Anne offered. "As is fatalism. But if Mr. Grant is truly doing well, I don't see why you have to rush anything, Harry. You just spent a fortune on catering a dinner that you had to give away, which you do not want to have to do again if you need to cancel. I mean, I support food kitchens, but I'm not sure the best donations are stuffed snapper and risotto."

"I heard the wedding cake was a big hit, though," Molly said. "What do you think, Helen? Can you officiate here later in the month?"

"I'm sorry, but the only date I could handle would be next weekend. After that, I'm tied down to events in the Taos area until mid–January."

"Molly's baby is due then," Anne said.

december wedding

Molly sighed and gestured toward Harry. "Tell me honestly what you want to do. We can have it here next weekend." She gestured toward her publicist. "Celia will crack the whip."

"Well, about that." Celia looked up from her phone, which she had been frowning at the last few minutes. "I'll be glad to line–up vendors, but we're going to have to get different people than last time." She moved uncomfortably in her chair in Molly's sunny kitchen. "It looks like one of the businesses we used before ratted us out."

"About what?" Harry and Molly asked in unison.

Celia held up her phone. "Your favorite rag of a tabloid, *The Daily Post*, just put up a story on their website that your wedding to Cruz was called off Friday at the last minute. They have photos of the cake being unloaded at the mission food kitchen. Twitter is exploding with fan outrage that you've been jilted by Cruz."

"Oh no." Molly paled.

Harry swore. Anne and Helen exchanged shocked glances.

"How can they print an out and out lie?" Molly asked. "I mean, they've printed 95% false stories before, but this is 100% inaccurate as to the people involved." Molly looked at Harry. "Where did Cruz say he was going this morning?"

"He went to Shar's house to check things are okay while she's away." Jesse's mother's house was in Carpentaria, twenty minutes away. "He took Marta and Jesse with him," Harry added.

"I need to call and warn him about this," Molly said. "Crap. Celia, get Artie and have him call that fish wrap and threaten to sue them, or bomb them or something. Who can you get a hold of that I can talk to and correct this story?"

Celia took her phone back from Molly. "*ET* and the network morning shows. And *The View* is always ready to talk about your life. But you're going to have to put out a statement." She grimaced. "Harry and Jackson will need to be identified as the couple who were getting married. I know you were trying to avoid that."

Molly rested her hand on her belly. "Yeah, that's not working out so well." She looked at Helen. "Harry is my half-brother. Anne gave me up for adoption when she was unmarried and sixteen. It's a family secret I've tried to keep private the last couple of years, but some press people have gotten the scent and are snooping around."

"Well, thank you for filling me in," Helen said. "I'm sorry if things are going public that you wanted to keep private. However, may I say, since I have met all you folks, you seem very much a loving and supportive family. I can't see where it would hurt to be revealed."

"Thank you. We are," Molly said. "And the only thing that hurts me is that they have no say in this. I hate putting my loved ones in the public eye just because of who I am."

"What jerks," Harry said. "I see why Cruz gets so upset. It makes you feel helpless."

"You are helpless in these cases." Molly reached out and patted Anne's hand. "I hope you don't mind me giving such a blunt overview of the past to Helen."

"Oh please, that's fine." Anne's usual, calm demeanor was in place. "And I don't care a bit about the story coming out, either."

"Really? We'll see how you feel after you're ambushed at the grocery store." Molly turned to Celia. "Okay, do a press release, short and sweet. Name Harry and Jackson as the couple who were getting married, but don't say anything except, they are dear friends of mine." She blinked. "It won't help anything for a few days until the tweet hounds die, but the internet celeb sites will pick something else up and run with it soon enough. We'll just have to wait them out."

"Why don't I just call *The Daily Post* and tell them it was me and Jackson who were getting married, and that we had a family emergency?" Harry asked. "I've got some press contacts, too." Harry was a make-up artist who worked primarily on Broadway, but he knew several people in the media business. "We won't have to mention anything about our connection to you. It might get them to drop the story."

"No, Harry, don't get involved. Jackson's family will have people at the hospital if you call." Molly sipped her now cold tea. "We could have some out on the lawn by noon today. Celia, can you also please call the Santa Barbara PD and ask them if they'll do an extra patrol this next week?"

"Yes, I will. But maybe you should could call Diane Kinsey," Celia said suddenly. "Her show is on tonight, as a matter of fact, and I bet she'll do a promo for your upcoming interview. She'd probably give a minute on–air to put out the real story if you asked her to."

Molly chewed her lip. "I don't know. We haven't seen the final cut of her interview with me. I'm not sure I want to start horse–trading with that woman right now."

"Those freaking leeches." Harry got up and started pacing, glancing out the kitchen window to check if anyone was there. "I'm going to call Jackson and tell him we'll just get married where his mom and dad live. New Mexico allows gay marriage. We'll just get married in the Los Alamos town hall."

"Don't rush into that decision," Molly said. "We can still reschedule it here. We'll do it right before Christmas, although we'll have to find someone other than Helen to do the service. Would Jackson go for that?"

"I don't know. But I'm pissed we already caused all this mess, Molly," Harry said. "You've got a new movie coming out and the baby's due next month. I hate that we're contributing more stress to your life."

"You're not what's causing my stress. I wanted to have your wedding here. This was my error. I should have realized that my house is too big a target. We should have had it someplace more discreet."

"Excuse me," Helen said. "I'd like to make a suggestion for you to all consider."

Everyone turned to the diminutive minister. "Why don't you all come to Taos for the holidays? We can have the wedding at Molly's home, which I understand is less than a mile from mine. I have three empty bedrooms and would be glad to put some of you up for a night or two, if Molly's place is not big enough. It will be quiet, away from the press, and near Jackson's parents. And Cruz mentioned you were considering going there for a week at Christmas." Her eyes twinkled. "Sorry, if he wasn't supposed to tell me that."

"Cruz would like that, wouldn't he, Molly?" Anne asked. "He was telling me on Thanksgiving that his favorite place in the world was his Aunt Rosa's house in the desert. Eric and I could drive together and help you set things up."

"Wow. I'd love that," Harry said. "We'll cut down the guest list to just family. We can throw a reception for our New York friends on New Year's Eve and announce we got married."

Molly felt a rush of adrenaline as the ideas bounced around the room. "I'll have to check with my doctor, but I'll still have three weeks plus before the baby is due. He said I could fly if it was a short trip. Taos is only two hours from LA."

"We'll charter a plane," Celia said. "Take everyone at once. How many from here?"

Molly named the group. "Maybe you could come too for a couple of days, Celia?"

Celia beamed. "I'd love to."

"Great. Then book a flight for a dozen. My place in Taos has three bedrooms, so we might take you up on your offer and put a couple of folks with you."

Helen clapped her hands together. "Excellent. I know my son Jim and his wife are going to be at my place for Christmas, but I have two bedrooms to spare."

"Thank you so much, Helen." Molly blew Harry a kiss. "See, all fixed. And we can keep this a secret. I'm sure we can."

"Shall we book a restaurant for a reception afterwards?" Celia asked.

"No. I have a great big table that can handle twelve in the living room, and a big river rock fireplace we can use for the wedding. We'll bring food." Molly grinned. "How's that sound, every one?"

"Doable. We will have turkey, ham, and sides. I'd like to invite John too, if you don't mind," Anne said.

"Of course. Sorry, of course include him, Mom." Harry sat back and folded his arms across his chest. "Does the press know about your house in New Mexico, Molly?"

"I don't think I've ever seen it featured in an article about me, and I know I've never mentioned it. Do you think Jackson's folks can come over for the day from Los Alamos? It's only about an hour drive."

"Yes, it sounds brilliant," he said. "Reverend Helen, fabulous idea."

She pointed upwards. "Divine inspiration. And while you are all there, I hope you'll make a private visit to my school. The kids would love to meet a movie star."

"I'd love to, Helen," Molly said. "Cruz told us what a wonderful job you folks are doing. How many children are you educating?"

"We have over a thousand refugees in six locations. The school in Taos is the biggest with two hundred."

"Cruz said you're doing amazing things." She turned to Anne. "She's taking in the immigrant children and working with Customs to find temporary homes for them. While they wait, local teachers who've donated time teach the kids English and other subjects."

"Think global, act local." Anne beamed. "I love it when people find ways to do that. Help the folks in your own backyard first, and that helps the world."

"That's it exactly, Anne," Helen said.

"Harry, you call Jackson and run it all by him. Celia, you'll take the lead?" Molly asked.

"Yes. I will call the charter folks and juggle a couple of press things you are scheduled to do for the new movie the week before Christmas. But it's a go, as far as I'm concerned. What date do you want for the wedding?"

Harry was looking at the calendar on his phone. "How about December 23rd? That way everyone can fly back out the 24th and leave Cruz, Molly, and Jesse to have a quiet holiday."

"Great. I have a press conference on the 21st, so we'll go down on the 22nd, Celia," Molly said. "I'll check with the doctor, but I'm sure a short flight on a charter will be fine. Cruz will be thrilled we're spending Christmas in New Mexico."

"You and Cruz can disappear off the LA and New York radar for a couple of weeks. That'll quiet the rumor mill down, too." Celia looked at her phone and raised her eyebrows. "But right now, I need to jump into the 'Cruz dumps Molly' story. I've already got 44 text messages waiting." She met Molly's eyes. "Including one from Ben Delmonico."

"Crap. Well, don't tell my ex–husband anything except to lose your phone number. I refuse to be cast as a victim to be pitied again, although, the ex–husband who made me one, seems more than eager to get a little more publicity." Molly got up slowly, pressing both hands into the small of her back. "Let me go call Cruz. I don't want him hearing he's left me on the radio." She shook her head. "He doesn't react well to this kind of crap, as we all know."

She walked out and Celia sighed. "That's an understatement."

# # #

"The rumor that you and Cruz broke up is still ricocheting around the media. I think you're going to have to sit down with someone for an interview," Celia said.

Celia, Artie Stein, and Molly were ensconced in the den of Molly's house. The Christmas tree was up, even though they were scheduled to be gone for the holidays, because Molly did not want to forego the fun of decorating the house.

december wedding

Molly turned from where she was standing in front of the fireplace. She held four Christmas stockings in her hand, the last one without a name, just the word *baby* stitched temporarily into the velvet. "I'm not doing it. New York is too far for the morning shows, and Cruz has insisted we aren't going to do another interview here at the house."

"You could do it by phone," Artie said. "Or Skype?"

Celia and Molly both shook their heads. "Those satellite things don't go over well," Celia said. "It looks too desperate."

"And I'm not desperate," Molly said. "I'm just sick of this! Maybe we could just put some photos of me and Cruz on *Instagram*."

"Would Cruz agree to that? Maybe include Jesse?"

Molly pursued her lips. "No, we're not allowing Jesse to be photographed, but Cruz might agree to have one of the two of us by the fire with my big belly prominently displayed." She patted her mid-section as it felt like the baby did a lap of freestyle backstroke. "That should convince people it's not an old photo."

"No, I think if you're not on TV live somewhere, people are still going to wonder," Celia said. "They want to see you and Cruz interacting."

"How about you two go out to a local place for dinner?" Artie said. "We'll tip off the local Santa Barbara paper."

"Maybe." Molly sighed and hung up the stockings, embroidered by Cruz's Aunt Rosa as an early Christmas gift to them this year.

Mi familia.

She turned from the mantle. "Let's just leave it, Celia. Let people think what they want, if they are really thinking about me at all. Concentrate on Friday's press conference for the movie, okay? Then, we'll sneak away to New Mexico, the baby will come in January, and the press will be chasing new stories."

"Did you decide about releasing the baby's first photos yet?"

"No. I think we should just quietly post it ourselves."

"*HELLO Magazine* has offered a million for your favorite charity."

"I know. Cruz likes that idea, particularly if we can get some of the money to Helen Nunez's organization, but I'm still thinking about it."

Celia grabbed her things. "Okay, boss. I'm off to my office. Can I do anything else for you?"

Artie stood up also, an unlit cigar in his hand. "I'll be at the press conference. I think Diane Kinsey is going to be there, too. Her office called and asked if you'd give her a few minutes privately."

Celia stopped at the doorway. "Why didn't they call me?"

"I don't know. Think something's up?"

"Maybe." The publicist scowled. "Feels like an end run if you ask me."

"Idiots," Molly said. "Artie, let Celia call Diane back and say I'll talk to her. But tell her no cameras, no sound bites. Just her and me for five minutes."

"Do you think it's about your relationship to the Sullivan family?" Artie asked.

"I have no idea. But I'll handle it." Molly's stress level ticked–up a notch and she wondered what kind of angle Diane Kinsey was playing with this request.

chapter seven

Cruz drove Molly into Beverly Hills for the press conference for her new movie, which was set to be released December 26th. They left early the morning of December 21st so Molly could get the hair and make-up treatment before the noon press event.

Artie, Celia, and Molly's agent, Sheila Gilles, were waiting in the suite for them. Cruz was edgy, as always, but seemed to Molly to be trying very hard to stay calm, knowing full-well that when he was uptight, it stressed her out.

"Hey, Cruz," Artie said. "Let's go down to the pool while Molly's at the press conference."

"I didn't bring a bathing suit," Cruz said. "And it's not that warm out."

"They have suits. And the pool is heated in December. It might be California, but the Beverly Hills Hotel knows its stuff."

"Why don't you go, Cruz?" Molly was sitting at the table with a cup of tea, while people buzzed around her. JoJo, her friend and go-to makeup expert was expected any minute, along with Laru, Molly's hairdresser.

"You know you hate to see the magic happen." She lifted up a lock of hair. "And since I'm not dying any of this for awhile, it's going to take a lot of magic to get my hair looking presentable."

Cruz touched her cheek. "You look beautiful."

"Molly, I need you to talk to Tina Brown in ten minutes. Can you do it?" Sheila put her cell against her ample breast and looked quizzically at Cruz. "Are you even better looking than the last time I saw you?"

Cruz grinned, a slight flush on his face. He had never gotten used to Sheila's ways, though he liked the brash New Yorker. "You don't get out enough if you think I'm good looking," he said.

"Sheila gets out plenty, and yes, he is better looking every day. It is totally not fair." Molly turned to Celia. "Yes, I'll talk to Tina."

Molly made a shooing motion with her hand at Cruz. "You need to leave before JoJo and Laru get here. They're all a bit too aggressively in love with you, and I'm feeling like a blimp."

"*Senora* is *loca*." He crossed his arms. "Everyone knows I've only got eyes for you."

"Hold that thought." She smiled. "Please go with Artie. I'll meet you back here about one thirty, and we'll have lunch in the room before we drive back. Work off some of that energy in the pool, okay?"

"I will. Don't forget to drink your water, okay?" He winked at Sheila, nodded at Celia, and followed Artie out of the room. Fifteen minutes later, he and Artie were ensconced in one of the private cabanas, ordering drinks and snacks from room service.

"How you feeling these days, professor? College kids still the same brats as ever?"

"I've got good students, Artie. They are sharper than ever. I need to work to keep up with the questions they ask about the material. I'm teaching Modern American poetry next semester. I need to do more homework."

"Your memory's recovered almost completely, Molly said." Artie lit his cigar and took a huge puff. "You've worked hard to get your old self back, *hombre*. I'm proud of you."

"Thanks, Artie." Cruz had thanked Artie several times over the past two years. The attorney had helped him through legal troubles and a custody battle with Jesse's mother, but most of all, he'd helped keep Cruz steady as he fought his demons after the motorcycle accident that nearly killed him four years ago. "I'm coming back to UC Santa Barbara to teach next semester."

"Molly told me that. You think you guys are going to settle here, then, after the baby?"

"I'm hoping Molly will take a break for a couple of years and we'll stay there. You know that. But she can still be close enough to LA to come down if she wants to."

Artie nodded. "She's going to be in demand more than ever after this picture comes out, Cruz. You know that, right?"

"I know. But I also know she's ready for a break, Artie. And her life is going to change when she has that baby. Caring for her child will be more important to her than any new movie project."

"I think you're right there." Artie pulled out his phone and began scrolling through the messages.

Cruz stretched out on the well-padded lounger and patted his chest, willing himself to relax. He'd considered bringing Jesse with them today. He should have. His son would have loved to play in a pool the size of a small lake.

He worried sometimes about Jesse and his exposure to Molly's wealth and lifestyle. Although she always kept things low key and casual, it had to affect the kid at some point.

Cruz exhaled deeply as the sun pounded his body. This wasn't his life, this extravagant, pampered existence available to celebrities like Molly Harper, but every once in a while he admitted to himself how seductive it was.

"Mr. Stein, I have a message for you," a bellman said beside him.

"That's Mr. Stein next to me." Cruz pointed, not opening his eyes.

"What the hell is this?" Artie took the folded piece of paper from the hotel porter. "Pretty old school, getting a note. Think Julia Roberts is here and wants me to meet her?"

All three men chuckled.

"What is it?" Cruz looked over at Artie, shielding his eyes from the sun.

Artie buttoned his shirt up. He handed the bellman a tip, and the man bowed his head and hurried off. "Celia wants me to come up to the suite," the attorney said. "Something about the Premier site contract being screwed up."

"Why didn't she just text you?" Cruz asked.

"Who knows? Probably wanted to be sure I didn't ignore her. I don't text, and I turn the damn phone off all the time. Drives the girl crazy." He grinned. "Don't let some starlet take my seat. Molly will kick my ass. I'll be back."

"Right." Cruz grunted and rolled over onto his stomach. A couple of minutes later, someone sat down next to him.

"Cruz? How are you man?"

Cruz opened his eyes. For a moment he thought he was hallucinating. Unfortunately he wasn't, as the last person on earth he wanted to see was beaming a movie–star smile at him.

"How you doing, guy? I heard you'd recovered from the accident. You look great." Ben Delmonico, Molly's ex–husband continued to hold out his hand for Cruz to shake.

"What are you doing here, Ben?" Cruz grabbed his shirt and pulled it on.

Ben dropped his hand. He was dressed all in white, including a porkpie hat with a pink hatband.

Cruz couldn't see the actor's eyes behind his opaque *Raybans*, but he knew they were staring at him.

"I'm meeting some people here for lunch. What are you doing here?"

"I'm waiting."

"For Molly? Is she here, too?" Ben took off his shades and glanced around the pool area. "You two are back together, then? I was really upset when I read a couple of weeks ago that your wedding got canceled."

Cruz stood and crossed his arms over his chest. "It wasn't our wedding."

Ben got up and faced Cruz. Though Ben was shorter and thinner by forty pounds of muscle, the actor took a slightly menacing pose and leaned toward Cruz. "That's your story and you're sticking to it, right? I get it, buddy. Believe me. I've lived with a pregnant woman. It's amazing any man hangs around these bitches when they're carrying a kid around in their belly. I mean, we're the ones who are sexually deprived for six months. I don't know why they get all the sympathy."

Cruz flinched. "See you, Ben." He turned and blindly walked toward the hotel, not sure which suite Molly was in, but he knew it was dangerous to be within an arm's length of Molly's ex.

"Hold up!" Ben grabbed his shoulder. "Come on, *amigo*. You don't have a beef with me. Molly's the one who chose me over you, but that was a long time ago. I didn't force the girl. Believe me, she was eager to be Mrs. Ben Delmonico. Look what it did for her. It made her."

"Let go of me." It was hard getting words out, and even harder to stay calm, Cruz was so angry.

"Or what?" The actor flashed his brilliant capped teeth. "You're worried Molly still has a thing for me, aren't you? Wondering if maybe she wishes she'd stayed with me? She would have, if Daniela hadn't been so careless and got herself knocked up."

Cruz's fist clenched. "If you say another word, you're going to regret it, Ben."

The actor smirked, but he dropped his hand. "You've wanted to take a punch at me ever since I married Molly. Why? Afraid you don't measure up, Cruz? Did your little motorcycle accident impair more than your brain? Maybe you're worried that bun in Molly's oven isn't even your kid? I heard a few rumors about her and Ryan when they were filming..."

Ben didn't get another word out.

Cruz punched him square in the nose, and the actor tumbled backwards. His feet upended as his ass whacked the pool deck, and both shoulders landed with a thud.

Two women screamed.

Three men in hotel uniforms came running over.

When Cruz turned toward the yelling he was immediately blinded by a blizzard of flashing lights. He put his hand up to shield his eyes.

He'd never seen the two men standing at the edge of the heavy foliage bordering the pool, holding cameras. But he saw them now. While his first thought was that he was glad he'd punched Ben Delmonico in his fake face, his second was that he'd blown it big time.

Regret swelled inside as he realized immediately that he wasn't really the target of this cheap publicity stunt. It was Molly who'd been set-up.

It was Molly whose life was going to be fodder for gossip once again in headlines everywhere, because he still hadn't learned to keep his mouth shut or his temper under control.

# # #

"Thanks so much for giving me five minutes, Molly." Diane Kinsey was waiting inside the small room Celia had arranged for their meeting. She sat down on the sofa and patted the cushion. "Come sit."

Molly walked to the chair across from the journalist. "I'll sit here. Easier to get out of this chair than a sofa."

Diane's eyes widened as she gave Molly a full body sweep. "You look stunning, as always, but wow, yeah, you're way bigger than a couple of weeks ago. When's your due date?"

"Not long now," Molly said. "So what's up, Diane?" She took a swig from a bottle of water. Her phone began to vibrate in her jacket pocket, but she ignored it.

"Right to the point? Okay then. I'm sure you want to get home and rest those ankles." Diane leaned forward, cupping her hands around her knee, her long, slender legs, and *Manolo Blahnik* clad feet offering a shot worthy of a leg model. "I just wanted to see how you're doing. I'm hearing you and Cruz are back together?"

"No comment."

Diane drew back. "Wow, really? I mean, I read your press release saying the break-up story was bogus, but I assumed that just meant you'd patched things up again. Don't you want to give me a quote like, "We're still in love and happily looking forward to our baby's impeding birth" or "We're getting married in January?" Diane grinned like a baby barracuda. "Come on, you already gave me the scoop that Cruz is your baby-daddy. I'd be delighted to help you out here."

"I'm sure you would be. But I have no comment, Diane." Molly stood up just as her cell again vibrated. "If that was what you were after, you should have said so when you reached out to Celia. You know I'm not going to say anything more about the fake *Daily Post* story. Or about Cruz."

Diane stood up, too. "Oh, Molly, I'm sorry you're feeling defensive. But I get it. Please sit down for a minute, though. I have something else I want to ask you."

Molly remained standing. She squinted at her phone. It was almost time for the press event to start. "I really need to get outside. Celia's been calling me..."

"I'll make it quick. How do you feel about adoption?"

"I think it's a wonderful thing," she said smoothly, although she squeezed the water bottle so hard it squeaked. "Why do you ask?"

"Well, I wanted to speak about your brother, Jason, and his adoption in my intro piece. I wondered what your take is on how your parents, long before it was so popular, came to adopt a boy from Korea. Couldn't they have more children after you were born?"

"No comment." Molly's cheeks reddened.

"Would *you* ever consider adopting a child?"

"Where are you going with this, Diane?"

"What do you mean?" She had a puzzled expression on her face, but her eyes were full of cunning. "I just want to hear your feelings. So many Hollywood actresses adopt; Angelina, Madonna, Charlize, Sandra Bullock..."

"They are all very admirable women, but I need to go get ready for the press conference now." Molly took a step toward the door. Suddenly it opened, and a white-faced Celia stood there, her mouth a tight, straight line.

"Molly, I need you. *Now*."

"What's wrong?" Diane said before Molly could get the same question out.

Celia gave the newswoman a look that could have killed her, if such things were possible. She put her hand on Molly's elbow and guided her out of the room.

"Don't say anything. Just walk with me. We're going to take the elevator to the parking garage," Celia whispered.

"Why? The press conference..."

"You are not going. Just walk."

Molly felt physically sick. She kept her eyes straight ahead and her face calm as they made their way down the hallway. If Celia was leading her away from a press conference and intent on getting her off the hotel grounds, something terrible had happened.

She swallowed as they turned the corner. "Is anyone hurt," Molly whispered, fears about Jesse, her brothers, and then Cruz, throbbed on and off like a traffic light inside her head.

"Cruz is in police custody," Celia hissed, so low Molly wasn't sure she heard her right.

"What?"

Celia repeated the news and smacked the elevator door, which opened immediately, and pulled Molly inside. As the doors closed, the two women turned toward one another.

"What the hell happened?" Molly demanded.

Celia took off her glasses and rubbed her eyes. "Cruz and Ben Delmonico had words. Cruz hit Ben, and he folded like a cheap umbrella. In full view of a couple of TMZ photographers."

december wedding

"Shit," the two women said in unison, as the hotel elevator slowly dropped to the basement.

chapter eight

It took Molly and Celia three hours to get from Beverly Hills to Montecito. They stopped for food at an In–N–Out Burger, and twice more so Molly could pee, the whole time fielding incoming calls and texts.

Celia drove.

Artie called an hour after they left the hotel and said he and Cruz were still at the police station, but that Cruz wasn't going to be arrested, because Ben wasn't hurt badly and had refused to press charges.

CBS, NBC, and Fox news each called Celia asking for a comment on the 'fist fight between Molly Harper's ex-husband and ex-boyfriend'.

ABC and CNN called Molly's phone and asked her to confirm reports she'd gone into labor after trying to break up a brawl.

Anne called Molly and asked if there was anything she could do.

Harry called Molly and bellowed through the speaker in her cell phone, "What the hell was Cruz thinking?"

"I wish I knew the answer to that, Harry, but I don't," she said.

"Well, this sucks, and I'm not going to give you any more stress. I talked to Jackson, and we've decided to go ahead with the marriage plans, but we'll do it without you. You stay in Santa Barbara."

"Oh, no, you don't, little brother," Molly yelled back. "I'm not missing your wedding because Cruz acted like a jackass. And neither is anyone else. I'm flying down tomorrow with

Anne and bunch of other people. If anyone stays home, it'll be Cruz." Molly inhaled. "All is a go!"

Celia raised her eyebrows but said nothing.

Five minutes later, the publicist stared down at the latest batch of texts, while Molly was in the bathroom at the mini-mart they stopped at in Ventura.

When Molly got back in the car, Celia swallowed hard. "I have it from two sources that Daniela's people are going to announce tomorrow that she and Ben have split. Jackie at the LA Times thinks Ben staged the fight with Cruz to drum up some sympathy, because Daniela's father is telling people that Ben was caught cheating on his daughter."

"What a cluster-f," Molly said. Her skull felt like it was full of sawdust. "But why bring Cruz and me back into the picture? Our history doesn't put Ben in any kind of favorable light, does it?"

"If he has a fight with Cruz, the press prints all that stuff again about you and Ben, and Daniela breaking up his marriage to you. My guess is Ben figures it will remind the public Daniela isn't a saint."

"You mean he staged a fight with Cruz to put Daniela on the defensive? Ben is such a dick. I mean, they have a child together."

"Ben thrives on publicity, good or bad. You know he wouldn't hesitate to use anyone or everyone in his life for his career." Celia narrowed her eyes as several new texts flooded onto her phone. "What really ticks me off is that Ben provoked this at the hotel where your press conference was going on. I think he did it to upstage you. He's so jealous you did the new movie without him."

"He must have guessed Cruz would be there," Molly said. "I shouldn't have let Cruz leave the suite. What I really don't understand is why Artie didn't stop the fight before it happened. He should have interceded the moment Ben walked up to them at the pool."

"Artie wasn't there."

"What? Where was he?"

Celia blinked. "He told me a bellman delivered a fake note to him, supposedly from me, to come up to the suite."

"Ben went to a lot of trouble to set this up," Molly said, her voice strained.

"Ben or *someone*." Celia frowned. "What happened with Diane Kinsey right before I came in?"

"She asked me a couple of lame questions about adoption. Then you knocked. That was about it."

The women stared at each other. "You think Diane sent the note to Artie? And deliberately pulled me aside to make sure Cruz was alone at the pool?"

"*The Daily Post* just tweeted Kinsey is sitting down with Ben tomorrow for an exclusive interview." Celia pulled off her glasses to clean them with the edge of her blouse. "If it walks like a duck, and quacks like a duck..."

"She's a freaking, lying, conniving witch of a TV host," Molly said through gritted teeth.

"It doesn't rhyme, but yeah, I think Diane's in this up to her neck." Celia started the car and put it in gear. "We're going to have to issue a statement."

Molly thought of a few, but none of them could be quoted.

#

Cruz walked into the bedroom in Santa Barbara that night at nine o'clock and found Molly in bed reading.

"Why didn't you answer your phone?" he asked. He stopped at the foot of the bed and crossed his arms.

"Why did you punch Ben Delmonico in the face in front of a news photographer?" She didn't look up from her book.

Cruz blinked. "He's a bastard."

"Yeah, well, tell me something new. Or something that would justify you almost being arrested, *again*."

"So this was my fault?"

She put the book down and looked at him. His expression reflected the strain of the day, as well as anger. At himself, she knew.

But knowing he'd done something stupid didn't do any good if he couldn't muster the self-control to walk away

december wedding

when provoked. "Yes. Hitting someone is assault, not chivalry. You could be in jail right now, Cruz. And if you were, that would be your fault, too."

He flushed deeply. "You don't know what he said."

"I don't give a damn what he said!" She threw her hands in the air and sent her book, her reading glasses, and a bottle of water flying.

Cruz crossed his arms. "He got what he deserved."

"No, he got what he wanted, Cruz. He played you like a master, and you gave him what he was looking for. Publicity."

Cruz stared at her. She could see he finally understood what had happened today.

"What was I supposed to do?"

"Walk away. You should have walked away, Cruz. Honestly, just when I think you've moved past your inability to control your anger, you do something like this. It makes me wonder if you're fully recovered from that head injury that robbed you of your ability to control your temper."

The silence grew more electric as the moments passed. Cruz glared at her. "I would have smacked him before I had an accident or a plate put in my head, *chica.* "I'm not going to stand by and listen when a man disrespects my woman. It's who I am. It makes me wonder if you've ever accepted that."

"Oh for God's sake." Molly put her hands on her face. She didn't know if she wanted to scream or laugh. She suddenly remembered the first time he'd called her his *woman*. She was seventeen and so besotted with the cook's son, she nearly fainted with desire.

Molly looked up at Cruz. "You've got to get past this, this being able to be provoked by *words*. We can't keep having the same argument."

"Maybe you need to stop working and stay home."

"What?"

"I know. You can't give up acting." He scowled and looked down at his feet. "I don't know how to fix this, Molly."

"If you'd just stop feeling that you have to defend my honor against people who don't matter at all to us! If we're ever going to get married…"

"*If?*" Pain flashed in his eyes and his face hardened. "I see. So when you said yes a couple of weeks ago, you meant yes, but only if I behaved?"

"Don't be ridiculous," she hollered.

"I'm not being ridiculous. I'm asking you to answer me. Are we still getting married?"

"Are you really asking me that again?"

The silence grew. "No," he said in a dead calm voice. "I'm never asking you that again."

"Good." As soon as she said it, Molly wanted to take it back, but it was too late.

Cruz began cracking the knuckles on his left hand. "I'm going to sleep in Jesse's room." He stalked toward the door.

"Are you packed? For tomorrow? We're leaving for New Mexico at ten a.m."

He turned toward her, slowly shook his head, and then disappeared into the darkened hallway. She heard a door close, and had no idea what to do next.

#

Celia had chartered a plane out of Santa Barbara into Taos Municipal airport, and the December 22nd, two-hour flight landed on a gloriously sunny afternoon without a hitch.

Molly, Marta, Jesse, and Celia, along with Harry, Anne, John Wright, and Rev. Helen Nunez disembarked to find Helen's son and his wife waiting to help transport the passengers, food, and presents to Molly's house.

Jackson was driving with his parents and two friends from Los Alamos and was expected in this evening.

Cruz had told Marta at five a.m. that he would be in Taos for the wedding tomorrow, but no one had a clue as to exactly how or when he would arrive.

"As long as it's not on a motorcycle," Molly replied curtly to Anne when she inquired how Cruz was traveling the eight hundred miles from California. Everyone knew the two of

december wedding

them had fought over the incident with Ben Delmonico, but all were sure it would blow over in time for Harry's wedding.

The charter was taking everyone but Molly, Jesse, and Marta back to California early Christmas Eve, and flying Jackson and Harry down to a resort in Baja for a short honeymoon, Molly's wedding present to her brother.

The mood was festive in the large van Celia had rented. It was a short ride to Molly's house, during which Helen Nunez gave the new visitors to the town a short history lesson. "We're at about 7,000 feet elevation, which is why the air is so clean and the sky so blue, but it makes it a bit of a challenge for those of us used to walking 5 miles a day, so beware."

"How long has the pueblo been here?" Harry asked, referring to the five–story compound Taos Pueblo, adobe group houses that had national landmark status.

"Best factual information is that native populations built it over a thousand years ago. It's the oldest continuously occupied building in America, with room for about two thousand people."

"The world's first condos," Marta said with a grin. "Common walls. I've got a friend who grew up there. She said it's dark but always cool inside. About one hundred fifty people still live there year–round."

"That's amazing," Anne said. "They've added plumbing and electricity to such old dwellings?"

"Yes," Marta nodded. "And television."

"What would we all do without internet?" Helen added.

I, for one, would be much happier, Molly thought.

A half hour after they landed at the airport, the van pulled into the drive at Molly's house. The one story pueblo style cottage was in the Taos Gorge area on a five–acre plot. It had golden scrubbed walls, red tile porches, and offered a majestic view of Wheeler Peak, the highest mountain in New Mexico at over thirteen thousand feet.

"I'm just a couple of miles down the road," Helen said, as she and her son, Jim, loaded back into their truck, leaving the van for Molly's group. She handed Molly a card. "Here's all the phone and address information. When you folks get sorted out, give me a call and I'll come get whoever is sleeping in our two guest bedrooms."

"This is all so kind of you." Molly gave Helen a hug. "Won't you come join us for dinner? Marta and Anne have brought about a thousand pounds of food with us for the next couple of days."

"We'll come for dessert, how about that?" Helen squeezed Molly's arm. "You get some rest and don't worry about entertaining. A wedding tomorrow and then a quiet Christmas here is just what the doctor ordered for you and that little one."

Molly rested her hands on her stomach. "I'm looking forward to that. I thought maybe one day after Christmas I could stop over at your school and meet the children."

"We'd love that, Molly. Is Cruz coming in tonight?"

"He'll be here for Harry's wedding," she replied. "That's all I'm sure of."

"Is he flying in?"

"I think he may be driving." Cruz did that whenever he was trying to make a decision about something, Molly knew. What worried her today was what, exactly, he was trying to decide. She'd done a lousy job of explaining why she was upset in the heat of their argument.

She regretted more than anything making reference to their getting married, although even now she wondered if the relationship of husband and wife would ever be the best fit for the two of them.

"I hope he gets in tonight. I heard on the local news there's a storm kicking up from the North. We've had some violent ones lately, and terrible visibility due to dust and/or hail. The airport has had to shut down. I wouldn't want anyone out on the roads during that."

"I'll let him know, Helen," Molly said. It would give her a good, neutral reason to call his cell, she thought. She waved as Helen and Jim drove off then went into the house.

december wedding

Inside was controlled chaos.

In the kitchen, Marta and John were unloading the bags and baskets of groceries, baked ham and turkey, homemade tamales and enchiladas, along with several boxes of ready to be heated finger foods for after tomorrow's ceremony. A small, two–tier, red–velvet wedding cake, Harry had baked himself, was unwrapped and sitting on the ancient planked hunt table. He was going to add the final icing and decorations himself in the morning.

"Ready for some soup and sandwiches?" Anne asked with a big smile. She stood next to the counter, a stack of plates, loaves of bread, and cold cuts arrayed in front of her. She'd brought vegetable soup that was bubbling on the stove and made Molly's mouth water.

"Yes. I'm famished. Did we bring onions for the sandwiches?"

"Always for you. Why don't you go put your feet up, Molly?" Anne said. "Harry's keeping Jesse and Andrew busy outside. Celia's out there too, her nose stuck in the phone."

"Thanks." She smiled at Maria and Eric, who were helping Marta load the refrigerators. "I appreciate everything you guys are doing."

"Holidays are family time. I'm so blessed we're all here together," Anne replied.

Molly headed for the bedrooms. She'd had the local woman who took care of the house come in this week and change all the linens, scrub up, and stock the two small bathrooms, as well as, leave a load of firewood and a small Christmas fir tree in the shed.

She'd planned to put it up to surprise Jesse on Christmas Eve and had brought a small package of ornaments from home to decorate it. They could have a family gift exchange before everyone left, with presents for Jesse from Santa on Christmas day. She knew Jesse was missing his mother. He'd cried when she called this morning, so she was going to work extra hard to make it a wonderful holiday for him.

Molly glanced through the French doors and saw Harry chasing Jesse and Eric's boy around on the patio. The kids were wearing miniature feathered headdresses and ere carrying small, gaily painted wooden bows and rubber arrows. *Evidently, Harry couldn't wait for Christmas to give out some presents*, she thought.

Molly checked the two small guest rooms, one with twin beds, the second with a queen, figuring Marta and Celia could share one and Anne and John the other. Everything was neat and tidy with fresh flowers and bottled water.

She took out a couple of quilts Norma made years ago, laid them on the beds, and then went into her own room. Feeling the strain of the day's activities, Molly collapsed on the bed and dug through her purse for her phone. There were several texts and messages, mostly from friends sending good wishes and asking questions about Cruz's beat–down of Ben Delmonico.

She shook her head as she scrolled through them. There were also messages from the director of her new movie, two from her brother Jason from Paris where he and his wife were spending Christmas, and one from Artie Stein asking her to call "about the Kinsey interview. I've seen the final cut. We've got issues to discuss".

But none from Cruz.

Outside the wind rattled the glass in the hundred–year–old window frames, and she remembered the caution from Helen Nunez about the weather. She pressed Cruz's number and waited.

He didn't pick up. She inhaled and left a message about the upcoming storm, then asked him to call and let her know what time he'd be in. "Jesse's doing great, but wants his Daddy here. I do too. Please, call me back when you get this."

She set the phone on the night table and unpacked her suitcase, lying the presents carefully in the top drawer of her bureau. She'd wrapped them all in green or orange tissue paper with gold ribbon, except the ones for Jesse, which she'd left to put out from Santa. Cruz had made him a small ride-on pony that was in a cardboard box in the kitchen, marked "Do Not Open".

She took off her shoes and lay down. She was having contractions daily now, not the real ones, but the Braxton-Hicks kind. Evidently baby Morales and her abdomen were practicing for the big day. She wished she could sleep for a couple of hours, but the smells from the kitchen were calling to her rumbling stomach.

"Molly, got a minute?" Celia stood in the bedroom doorway, her eyes huge behind her black-framed glasses.

"Sure." Molly patted the mattress next to her. "What's up?"

"I got an email from Artie. The Kinsey interview tape was delivered to him this morning. He watched it and wants to talk to you."

"Let's call him after lunch. I'm sure he's not going to like something Diane says about me, Cruz, or the fact she'll probably have photos from the poolside fight. Frankly, I just don't care anymore about the gossip she's going to shovel out there. I'm ready for some time off."

Celia pushed her glasses firmly onto the bridge of her nose. "Okay. But there's something in the interview we weren't expecting."

"What?"

"Kinsey's revealing the facts about you being adopted. She's naming Anne Sullivan as your mother. And Harry and Eric as your half-brothers."

Even though Molly knew that the most private of her past history might come out some day and had warned Anne about it, Celia's news hit her like a blow.

Protectively, she put her hands on her stomach. "Okay, let's call Artie right now. I want him to threaten to sue her. She can't have any proof. My birth certificate says Norma and Charles Wintz are my parents. California adoption laws are really tough."

"Kinsey's got an interview with a woman who has proof." Celia took a breath. "The woman worked in Charles Wintz's lawyer's office, and she's got an original copy of the adoption papers, signed by Charles and Norma Wintz one day after you were born. It's an original document with a big fat gold seal from the court." Celia sighed. "You're going to have to put out a statement."

chapter nine

Several hours later, Molly sat outside on the quiet patio, wrapped in two sweaters and a shawl, and stared up at a blanket of stars. She'd visited a hundred places in the world, but none was brighter. The combination of being high in the mountains and away from a big city amplified the effect.

She'd seen three shooting stars careen across the blackness, and had made a wish on two of them, but so far Cruz Morales hadn't appeared beside her, so evidently her requests weren't being heard.

The sounds of the van starting up in front of the house drifted back to her, as John loaded up Harry, Eric, and his family for the drive to Helen Nunez's house for the night.

Through the windows she watched as Anne and Marta were putting Jesse down for the night in the guest bedroom. She turned her eyes and saw Celia curled up in the big leather chair by the fireplace, furiously typing on her phone. They'd made a conference call to Artie, who had unhappily agreed with Molly's request to do nothing about Diane Kinsey until after Christmas.

Molly wasn't sure yet what kind of statement she was going to make. She wanted to come up with a way to thwart the ratings coup Kinsey was sure to get for her shocking revelations about Molly's personal history.

I have to tell Anne and the boys what's coming first. She did not have the heart to reveal they were about to be outed to the world as her blood relations, mostly because she didn't want to ruin the fun of Harry's wedding tomorrow.

While it wouldn't upset the Sullivans, it just didn't seem fair to her to have to inject Diane Kinsey's agenda into their plans.

Molly laid her head back in the ancient rocking chair and closed her eyes. *If I stayed here and never went back to California, pulled the plug on technology and turned off the phones, the TV and internet, cancelled Facebook and twitter and everything else Celia uses to spin information out there with, how long would it take before the world forgot about me?*

How long before no one would care who my lover, mother, or baby was?

Could I give–up everything I love about acting and the movie business in exchange for quiet, peace, and family?

"Penny for your thought, *chica*."

The baby did a somersault and sent a rippling shimmer across her belly. Her heart raced and Molly turned and reached out into the darkness for Cruz, who had materialized beside her, her fondest wish granted as if a fairy godmother had heard her thoughts.

"I'm so glad you're here," she murmured as he bent down and enveloped her in his arms. "But why didn't you call me back? I've been worried."

"Sorry, babe." His voice was weary. "I left my cell phone at home. I didn't realize it until I stopped in Arizona for gas. The pay phone there was dead, so I just said the hell with it and kept driving."

"I hoped you'd be here tonight. You must be exhausted."

"I'm glad I'm not sitting in that truck." He kissed her tentatively, taking both their emotional temperatures in the cold air of the night. "So what's going on? All calm here in the high dessert?"

"I wish, but of course something else has developed." Briefly, she told him about Diane Kinsey's incursion into her family heritage. "I haven't told any of them yet, because I don't want to put a damper on tomorrow for Harry and Jackson."

"You're going to have to tell them soon. Especially Jackson's parents, who don't know the family story, right? You don't want them to find out listening to the car radio if this leaks out."

"Damn, I forgot about the Grants not knowing." She hugged him closer. "You're being very calm about this."

"Are you surprised? I know how to handle things in a mature way." His tone was ruefully sarcastic, but there was still an edge of anger.

"Very funny," she said gently. "Do you want to talk some more about what happened at the hotel?"

He broke their embrace. "There's not much to say. I was wrong to hit Ben. But I'm not sorry. The only thing I'm sorry about is that it made you change your mind about our getting married."

"I think our being married might make things worse for you. You'll be more of a target for reporters."

"I know." He turned away, cracking his knuckles as he walked to the edge of the patio. "I did a lot of thinking while I was driving here. I want you to know, I meant it when I said I'm not going to ask you to marry me, ever again."

She swallowed hard and leaned against the railing for support. Her face flushed and she cleared her throat. "Does that mean you don't want to get married anymore?"

"It means what I want most is for you, Jesse, and our baby to be healthy and happy. I'm going to concentrate on helping make those things happen."

"You didn't answer my question." She knew she was pushing him, and she had no right to, but she couldn't help it. "You don't want to marry me anymore?"

Cruz put his hand on her face and tilted her chin up. "If you're ever ready, and believe in your heart that *I'm ready* to handle all that comes with marrying you, then you ask me. It's up to you now, Molly Harper."

"Cruz, I..."

He put two fingers gently on her lips. "Did what happened at the hotel change how you feel about me? About us."

She shook her head. "Nothing is ever going to change the fact I love you with all my heart."

"Well, then that's enough for right now." Cruz smiled at her for the first time since he'd arrived. He sat in the rocker next to her and pulled her onto his lap. "How's everyone holding up? Did Jesse do okay on the plane?"

"He was great." She snuggled closer. "But I want to say one more thing. I realize you were ambushed at the hotel, and I don't blame you for lashing out, but Ben can't hurt me. He can't hurt us."

"I know that now." He began to rock. "I know."

She laid her head on his chest. "It's unfair that we have to put up with that kind of crap."

"*All's fair in love and war*," he quoted. Cruz kissed the top of her head.

"Shakespeare?"

"Novelist Frank Smedley, 1840. Although, Cervantes wrote the same basic words a hundred times in *Don Quixote*."

She thought about her own knight errant, tilting at windmills on her behalf, and smiled in the dark. "Am I heavy on you, Professor Morales?"

"You're light as an angel."

"Yeah, right." She struggled to get off his lap and pulled her fingers through her wild hair. "Did you eat? There's enough food for a hundred truck drivers in the kitchen. Anne and your mother went nuts with provisions. Good thing I have that old refrigerator out in the garage plugged in. Prepare to gain ten pounds in the next week."

"Marta and Anne know how to *make some groceries*," he teased in a heavy accent. Cruz smiled, his earring glimmering like one of the stars against his tanned skin. "Come on, let's go eat something and then get you into bed. How are Jesse and Andrew getting along?"

december wedding

"Great. Jesse is so good at sharing his toys. He's going to be great with the baby."

"We'll see about that. I'm not sure *mejo* understands little babies cry all night."

"Babies cry all night?" Molly asked in a shocked voice. "No one told me that!"

They laughed and walked arm–in–arm into the house. Molly caught one more shooting star out of the corner of her eye, but she was done with wishes for tonight, more than content with the blessings she had.

# # #

"Harry Sullivan and Jackson Grant, with great joy I pronounce you partners in life, *for life*. May you treasure the love you each freely and joyfully pledge to one another for the rest of your lives. In front of these witnesses, and by the power vested in me by the great and glorious state of New Mexico, I pronounce you legally married." Helen Nunez, her pastoral vestments sparkling with gold and red over her white tunic, ended the ceremony with her hands uplifted.

Harry and Jackson kissed and embraced. Everyone clapped and yelled. Eric put his fingers in his mouth and did a wolf whistle that hurt everyone's ears. Jesse and Andrew ran in mad circles through the room, across the rug in front of the huge stone fireplace where the happy couple took turns hugging all in attendance.

"Keep filming, John," Anne whispered, and wiped tears from her cheeks.

"I'm getting it all. You are the most gorgeous mother of the groom I've ever seen, by the way." John nudged her shoulder, his eye glued to the lens of the small video camera. Cruz had entrusted him to film the events of the day.

"Thank you. You clean up very nice yourself." Anne moved around the living room, hugged Celia, then Marta, and Jackson's parents.

Molly turned from embracing Harry and hugged Anne tightly, her belly hard as rock under the pattered red and white silk dress. She'd chosen this one instead of the white satin dress she'd also packed because it felt more festive, and the other one looked too much like she was the bride.

Everyone was dressed in white or red with flowers in their hair or lapels on orders from Harry.

"Congratulations, Anne," Molly said. "What a happy day for all of us in this family."

Anne nodded, touched that Molly's words included them all in the same family. She smiled at her daughter's beautiful, famous face. "It is a glorious occasion. Thank you again for hosting us all here."

"Glad to do it." Molly's gaze roamed the crowd for a moment. Jackson's friends, the Hunters, were sitting with his parents at the dining room table. Celia, Maria, and Marta were uncovering food, while Cruz was opening bottles of champagne.

"John, could you get some film of that side of the room?" Molly asked. "I'd love a shot from outside on the patio into the house, too."

"Sure thing. Are you adding directing to your resume, Miss Oscar winning actress?"

"I've always wanted to direct, as a matter of fact, so make sure it's award-winning quality." Molly turned back to Anne. "I need to talk to everyone about something before the party breaks up, but I wanted to tell you first." She dropped her voice and took Anne's hand, leading her into the empty kitchen. "Diane Kinsey is going to report on her TV special that you're my mother."

Anne's expression moved from joy to surprise to anger in the course of the next minute as Molly told her the details. "I was going to wait until the morning of the 26th and call everyone, but I thought it would be better to tell Jackson's family in person, since they are now related to me. In case it leaks before the show."

"They'll be thrilled, I'm sure," Anne said. "But I'm so sorry, Molly. For your having to put up with this, this intrusion."

"I've come to terms with it. I understood a long time ago that no personal information is off–limits when you live in the public eye like I do." She sighed. "Just be warned, you'll be fielding more than a few calls and probably a visit or two from the media for the next few weeks."

"I'm relieved our relationship is coming out. But I hope you understand that I decided a long time ago I have no intention of talking to anyone about you."

"Whatever feels right to you is fine with me," Molly said. "Celia pointed out to me something you should think about, though. You're a great role model for young girls. What you did giving me up for adoption was selfless, and very hard." She patted her stomach. "I understand that now in a way I never did. I'd do anything to make sure this one has a great life."

Anne was suddenly dizzy with emotion. This was what she had been hoping to hear some day from Molly. Not forgiveness for giving her up all those years ago to Norma and Charles Wintz, but for understanding that she had acted not from shame or fear or pressure. But from love. *Love for her*.

"Thank you, dear daughter," Anne murmured.

"You're welcome, mother." It was the first time Molly had ever called Anne that. Both immediately began crying and hugged each other tightly.

Anne patted the pocket of her jacket and pulled out a small envelope. "I wanted to give this to you privately this weekend, and now feels like the perfect time."

Molly wiped her eyes as Anne took out a small gold pin with a tiny blue enameled charm of the Virgin Mary dangling from it. She handed it to Molly.

"This was pinned on your tiny gown in the hospital the day you were born. When they brought you to me, I hugged and kissed you, and then they took you away. That night the nurse gave the pin to me to keep."

Tears streamed down Anne's face and her throat was so tight she could hardly talk. "I kept it all these years, just for myself, but somewhere in my heart I was hoping I could one day give it to you for your own little one. It blessed you with a wonderful life. And hopefully it will be lucky for your own little baby."

Molly clasped the memento against her heart. "Thank you, this means more than you know. I'll treasure it."

"Hey, what's going on here?" Cruz rounded the corner and came upon the emotional scene. His eyes were serious though his face was wreathed in smiles.

He was wearing a crisp white Mexican wedding shirt in honor of Harry's dress code and looked as handsome as Jackson, if a little rougher around the edges. "So, the women folk are off crying in the kitchen? Come on you two, we're not at a wake, we're at a wedding. Let's see some smiles." He circled his strong arms around both of them as they wiped their eyes.

"We need to do some eating now, no more tears!" Cruz scolded.

Anne smiled and Molly handed her a tissue, and the three of them returned to the living room. After an enormous lunch, and the wedding cake was cut and served, Eric gave a toast to his brother and Jackson.

Cruz followed, ending with "Congratulations, *mi familia!*" Everyone clapped and hooted.

Marta took Jesse off for his bath and Molly made her way to the head of the dining table. "I want to make a little speech, too."

In a voice hoarse with the emotional roller coaster the day had been, she told the Grants that Anne Sullivan was her birth mother, and that Harry and Eric were her half-brothers. She explained that this news was newly revealed to all of them in the last couple of years. "So I was given the gift of a second mother and two more brothers, and now I've got Jackson Grant in my family, too. And you all have me!"

"You mean we're related to a movie star?" Jackson's father asked the room.

december wedding

"I knew it!" Mrs. Grant shook her finger at Jackson and Harry. "Didn't I say more than once I thought Harry and Molly Harper looked alike?"

"You did. But you said I was more beautiful, right Lily?" Harry quipped.

They all roared at that.

The Grants got up and hugged Molly, and everyone started proclaiming their displeasure about Diane Kinsey and the questionable journalism practices that would allow her to reveal such sensitive personal information, even though Molly hadn't authorized her to do so.

Helen Nunez shook her head and said they should all write letters to the network, but Molly told them all to celebrate the news of their day, and not let a TV show ruin anything.

At eight o'clock, after more coffee and wrapping-up of leftovers, Harry and Jackson and his parents and friends headed out to the cars. The Grants and the Hunters were driving back to Los Alamos that evening, and Harry and Jackson were spending their wedding night at a Lodge in Taos.

Helen Nunez also left with Eric's family, telling them all she'd be over for Christmas brunch tomorrow morning before everyone flew off to return to California for Christmas.

An hour later Molly, Cruz, and the rest of the party settled in for one last night cap. Cruz lit the fire, and they all stared into it, retelling stories from the party and past holidays.

Molly started to nod off. Her lower back ached and her legs felt particularly heavy, but she didn't want to move off the sofa where she was wedged between Cruz and Harry. "It was a perfect wedding," she said.

"It was." Harry lifted his eyebrows dramatically. "So, when are we going to plan yours, sister dear?"

There was a moment of silence, and then Molly giggled. "*Someday, over the rainbow...* And for the record, I'll be just as pretty as you on my wedding day, Harry."

They all laughed again, and Cruz hugged her against him. It might be the most perfect night of my life, Molly thought, and closed her eyes and fell asleep.

# # #

Molly woke up seven hours later beside Cruz, feeling more refreshed and full of energy than she'd had for the last six months.

She crept out of bed. No one else was awake, even Jesse. She went into the bathroom and then the kitchen and started breakfast. By the time Marta and Anne got up, followed by Cruz and John, coffee was made, ham and bacon were ready on a platter, and a huge chili cheese egg dish Celia had brought was ready to eat.

"I know we're hosting brunch in a couple of hours, but I thought we'd all have something now. I know I'm hungry."

"Me, too" Celia said sleepily. "I don't know how I am, after the five pounds of food I ate yesterday, but I am." The young publicist sat down and handed Molly her plate.

Anne watched with silent speculation as Molly bounced around like superwoman, serving them all breakfast. "How are you feeling this morning? You look great."

"I feel amazingly good. Fabulous night's sleep. Just refreshed and full of energy. How are you?"

"Good. Must be the mountain air." Anne looked obliquely at Molly, who was wearing a sweatshirt of Cruz's over her nightgown. She was certain that Molly was carrying the baby much lower than she was yesterday. The baby wasn't due for almost a month, however, and Anne began to worry.

"So what's on tap, next?" Cruz held a huge mug of coffee, his plate of food already half-gone. "Is everyone coming back here with Helen?"

"Are we having presents?" Jesse said.

"Ah, *mejo*, you remembered about the presents."

december wedding

"Molly said that's one way to show someone you love them. I made you one, Daddy. All by myself."

"Did you?"

"He did," Molly said. "He's very artistic."

"Can I give it to you now?" Jesse asked.

"We should wait for the others, Jesse."

"No, let him give it to you," Molly said. "Sometimes early presents are the best. I always got one special present on Christmas Eve."

"Can I, daddy?"

Cruz nodded. "Okay, Jesse."

Marta and Celia made room for Molly between them, when the actress finally sat down to eat. Jesse came back into the kitchen carrying a tissue wrapped box with Daddy scrawled on the card. "I can't spell, but Molly drew Daddy on a paper, and I copied it."

"Good job." Cruz put down his coffee and opened the small package. Inside was a framed picture of three stick figures. A tall one with black hair. A smaller one in a dress with spiky yellow hair. Both held hands with a little one with brown hair. Beside them was a small bed–shaped box with a tiny stick baby in it. The stick baby had one blue ribbon and one pink ribbon on its cradle.

"It's our family," Jesse said. "We don't know what kind of baby it is. But it will be small."

Everyone laughed and applauded Jesse's drawing.

Suddenly Cruz took a small leather pouch from the pocket of his denim shirt and handed it across the table to Molly. "This is for you, *chica*. In the spirit of showing people you love them with gifts, this is my special gift to you this Christmas Eve."

Molly reached for it and met Cruz's eyes. She looked down and opened it. Inside was an exquisite sapphire ring with a diamond on either side, set into a gorgeous antique setting with scrollwork flowers etched onto the platinum sides.

"It's Nana's ring. You got it set with new stones for Molly," Marta said, covering her mouth as tears fell.

"*Sí, mamacita.*" Cruz looked at Molly. "My grandmother sold her diamonds to pay for my college. I never knew about that when she was alive. But Mama gave me the ring years ago and said I should use it someday. So I bought the blue stone for your eyes and the diamonds for Jesse and the baby."

Molly put the ring on her left hand and held it out. "It's exquisite, Cruz." Their gazes locked across the table. His words to her last night replayed in her mind, and she knew in her heart there would never be a man more perfect for her. "Will you marry me, Cruz Morales?"

Celia gasped and everyone else looked stunned. Cruz drew back in surprise. For a moment he looked like he might say no, but then his eyes brimmed with emotion. "Yes. Yes I will. Just tell me when."

For a moment no one said anything.

"Today!" Jesse yelled.

Cruz nodded. "Well?"

"Yes, how about today? You said people can get hitched the same day they get the license in New Mexico. We can drive over to Taos City Hall before they close. I'll wear sunglasses and a hat and scarf and we'll be in and out. Helen can marry us here after brunch."

"Holy mother, are you sure, Molly?" Cruz asked.

Anne started to cry and John and Marta hugged. Celia shook her head, smiling huge. "Oh my God," she said.

Molly got up and walked around the table. She wrapped her arms around Cruz's neck. "I'm sure. What do you think, Jesse? You sure you want to have another wedding today?"

He frowned, suddenly seized with worry. "Will Santa still come tonight?"

"Yes. Santa likes weddings. He'll still come."

"Then I say yes."

Everyone hugged everyone else. Molly and Cruz embraced. Jesse and a tearful Marta and Celia danced in a

december wedding

circle while Anne and John hugged and started organizing transportation for the sudden turn of events.

Three hours later the deed was done, and the bride and groom to-be walked into the house with marriage certificate in hand.

When Helen and Molly's brothers arrived a few minutes later for brunch, they found Molly Harper, movie star, standing in front of the fireplace dressed in white satin.

She was radiant, wearing red amaryllis flowers in her hair and a smile that would win an Oscar for happiest actress on earth, if there was such a category.

"Molly! What in the world is going on?" Harry asked.

"I told you I'd be a pretty bride, Harry Sullivan. Your sister is getting married today!"

chapter ten

Helen married them in a traditional, no frills recitation of the civil ceremony, where Molly and Cruz pledged to love, honor, and cherish each other until death.

Another feast was consumed, more champagne flowed, and Harry donated the top half of his wedding cake for the event. As people carried plates into the kitchen, Helen's son arrived to help with transporting guests to the airport.

"What's going on Molly?" Jim asked in amusement, staring at Molly's white dress and glowing smile.

"I'm a married woman now," she said.

"But don't anyone tell anyone else," Celia said. "I don't want the news showing up on Facebook." She turned to Molly. "I sent Artie an email saying you still didn't have an adoption story statement. He just called and said he'd sit tight, and that he's thrilled about the wedding. Says to tell you both *mazel tov*."

"You told him?"

"You didn't say I couldn't." Celia's eyes widened. "Should I not have told him?"

"Of course you should have told him. It saves me a call." Molly gave Celia a hug. "I'm so glad you were here with us."

"Me, too. How are we going to handle the announcement of the wedding? And photos?" Celia glanced at John, who seemed to have permanently affixed the camera to his face. "John, can you send the video to my email account so I can pick some shots to release."

"Wait a minute," Molly said. She took a breath, ordering her mind to succinctly spit out the plan she'd been formulating for the past few hours. "Celia, didn't you tell me that magazines would pay big bucks for the baby's photos?"

"Yes."

"What about for *exclusive wedding photos*?"

"Well, yes. Maybe not as much for when your baby is born, but *People, Hello Magazine,* or *Vanity Fair* would pay huge money for an exclusive."

"And I can have them directly pay the fee to a charity?"

"Yes."

Cruz was standing next to Molly and she squeezed his hand. "How about if you make a couple of calls right now and drum up some interest – keep it top secret and all that – about a breaking news story."

"You're going to do an interview about getting married?" Celia asked.

"No. I want Helen to do an interview. About performing the wedding."

"I don't understand," Helen said.

"I'm giving you the story, Helen." Molly's voice was suddenly all business. "Along with exclusive rights to some of the film John shot. And some photos. And you are going to sell the story, with Celia's help, to the first major publication that agrees to put the material up on their website the morning after Christmas. And that major publication will give you a nice big fat check for your schools."

"What?" Helen clutched her chest.

"That's a terrific idea, Molly," Cruz said.

"This is so generous." Jim hugged his mother. "Are you okay, Mom?"

"I can't believe this," Helen said. "Thank you Molly, and Cruz. This is so amazing."

"Molly, are you saying you want the story up *before* Diane Kinsey's interview airs?" Celia asked as she wrestled her cell phone out of her coat pocket. "*Before* the interview?"

"Oh, yes. *Before the interview.*" Molly chuckled and winked at Anne across the room. "I think Helen might upstage the story of my being adopted with my becoming Mrs. Cruz Morales, but you won't mind that, will you, Anne?"

"I think it's a brilliant idea," Anne said. "All's fair in love and war, right?"

Cruz and Molly looked at each other and burst into laughter.

#

Two hours later the winds were picking up and the sky was darkening ominously. John waved as he drove the van carrying Molly's family down the street toward the airport. The pilots had called and warned them they had to take off by four or risk being cancelled.

Celia and Artie brokered a deal in record time with *Hello* and *People* magazines to jointly break the wedding story on their website, with a special edition the following week. Helen and Jim headed home to sign and fax back the agreement that was waiting for them.

The final bid was over a million dollars for the photos and two fifteen–second clips of Molly and Cruz getting married, with a bonus photograph of Harry and Jackson and all of the Sullivan clan gathered around the wedding banquet the day before.

"So Helen Nunez will be breaking the story of your family connections before Diane Kinsey does," Celia had commented. "I'm sure she'll threaten to sue you about breaching your word about an exclusive."

"You think? Poor Diane. She won't win that one. Helen's story doesn't say a word about Cruz being the father of our baby." Molly hugged her publicist. "Have a lovely couple of days. We'll talk at New Year's okay?"

"Yes boss. Enjoy."

Molly shut the front door and sighed. All their guests were gone except for Anne and John, who at the last minute had decided to stay in Taos at an inn for the holidays.

"Please stay here with us," Molly had offered. "Jesse and Marta will be here."

december wedding

"No, you all enjoy your Christmas morning together. Maybe I'll come by tomorrow night though, and help Marta sort out the leftovers." Anne smiled. "I want to spend a little time alone with John, anyway."

"You must come for Christmas dinner, *mamacita*," Cruz insisted. "We want all our family that is here in town with us for the holiday."

Anne nodded happily, and she and John took Cruz's truck. "Okay, we'll see you tomorrow afternoon. Merry Christmas!"

"Merry Christmas!"

They spent the next hour putting up the fir tree and hanging the stockings Marta had remembered to bring from the house in Santa Barbara.

They sang Christmas carols, and Marta and Jesse made sugar cookies, which they all decorated for Santa.

Molly and Cruz went to bed a few minutes after Marta and Jesse, after filling the stockings and putting out presents from Santa.

"Time for bed, Mrs. Morales."

"Time to sleep, Mr. Morales," Molly answered. She held her ring up and saw the glittering lights of the tree reflected in the blue stone. "I so love this ring. I can't believe you kept a secret like this from me."

Cruz kissed her and then banked the fire before they crawled off to sleep.

At six–thirty a.m., Jesse hopped into bed with them, and by eight the presents were opened and Marta was preparing breakfast. Outside the light was muted, and the gorgeous crisp blue sky of Christmas Eve was replaced by a muddy gold, sand–filled wind that howled in the distance. Cruz frowned at the scene outside the French doors.

"I don't like not having transportation in this weather. I think I'll call John and Anne and have them drive over here now."

"What are you worried about?" Molly sat in front of the fire, a blanket over her legs. She was exhausted, her body heavy and slow, which she was sure was caused by yesterday's excitement.

"In case you haven't noticed, you're pregnant. And if something happened, I don't have any way of getting you to the hospital."

"You worry too much, Cruz." She handed him her empty glass. "Would you get me some water? I'm so thirsty."

"You haven't eaten anything, *chica*. You want some pancakes?"

She wrinkled her nose. "I'm really not hungry. I think I ate too much the last two days."

"You didn't have that much yesterday. You didn't touch the soup at dinner."

"I'm fine."

Cruz slanted his eyes at her and took her glass. "Stay put. Mama and I will handle dinner."

Molly stared outside at the brown air. It had grown nearly dark in the last half hour, and a low, scraping sound from outdoors unsettled her. She squinted and realized it was sand blowing against the windows.

Her cell phone made the odd, dying bee sound it made when the battery died, but she ignored it. The wedding story was signed, sealed, and delivered, thanks to Artie's and Celia's capable hands. It amazed her that, even on Christmas Eve, her publicist and attorney had been able to get through to decision makers and sew up the deal for Helen Nunez.

She was truly blessed with the people who helped care for her career, she thought. *Now if only someone could go to the bathroom for me.*

Molly rubbed her stomach with both hands and sighed. The Braxton–Hicks contractions had increased to a couple an hour the last two days, but as long as she didn't have more than four an hour, or they didn't increase in duration or intensity, her doctor and Lamaze teacher had told her it was normal.

december wedding

Slowly Molly got up and took three steps across the wide tile floor when she felt her water break.

She knew what was happening because she'd once researched a part for a film where she played a woman who went into premature labor. Molly blinked and stared at the floor as the amniotic fluid ran down her legs.

"Cruz!" she yelled, but he was already there.

He stood two feet away staring at her. "What's wrong?"

"My water just broke."

Cruz swallowed and set the glass down on the fireplace mantle. He picked Molly up in his arms and took her into the bedroom and laid her gently on the bed. "I'll call for an ambulance. Don't panic."

"I'm not panicking." She wasn't. She felt odd; light-headed but serene. Then she had a contraction so violent she gasped.

Cruz narrowed his eyes. He was staring at his phone, which said, *no service*. "Where's your cell?" he asked.

"On the sofa. But you're going to have to plug it into the charger. I think it just died."

Outside a boom echoed, followed by a horrendous crashing sound. The house shook and the lights went off.

In the other bedroom, Jesse woke up crying from his nap. Molly heard Marta comforting him in Spanish, and pictured them together in one of the twin beds. She swallowed and started to call out to them when another crash exploded, nearer to the patio. The sound of breaking glass made her sit up.

Cruz rushed into the room. "We lost two of those scrawny oaks beside the driveway. One of the windows in the kitchen just shattered from one of the limbs. Stay where you are, okay?"

"I will, but please go tell Marta what's happening. I heard Jesse crying."

Cruz left and came back a minute later. "I told Mama to stay put. Jesse's sleeping again and there are no trees near those windows in the other bedrooms." He looked across the room at the tall windows. "You doing okay?"

"Yes, I, oh my god," Molly clutched her stomach as a very strong contraction made her ache from head to knees. She did the breathing she'd been practicing for months, blowing out in measured small puffs.

Cruz knelt beside her. "I can't recharge your phone, and mine has no reception. I'm going to walk over to Helen Nunez's and borrow her car."

Molly shook her head. "You can't leave! Don't be crazy. You can't go out in this storm. If you don't go blind with the sand, you could get hit with one of the falling trees."

"Molly, you need to get to the hospital."

Just then the front door slammed. Cruz got up as John Wright called out, "Molly? Cruz? Where is everyone?"

"John, we're in here," Cruz called out.

A few moments later Anne Sullivan appeared at the bedroom door. Her eyes opened wide at the sight of Molly on the bed, her knees drawn up in pain. "So what's going on in here?"

"Molly's water broke."

"I think I'm in labor," Molly said on top of Cruz's explanation.

"Really. Okay. That's a nice Christmas present." Anne walked to the bed and motioned for Cruz to step aside. "How far apart are your contractions?"

"I don't know for sure. A few minutes."

Cruz walked over to John. "Does your cell work?"

"No. There's no reception in this storm," he said. "We tried to call you from the hotel, and when we couldn't get you, Anne said we better come." He nodded at Molly. "She was worried about you."

"We're going to have to put Molly in my truck and drive her to the hospital," Cruz said.

Molly yelped in agony and everyone turned to stare at her.

december wedding

"The visibility is really bad out there, Cruz. And the hospital is ten miles. I think we better stay here," Anne said.

Molly was panting. "I'm not getting in a car." She cringed again and grasped Anne's hand. "The contractions are coming fast. Way too fast, I think. Something must be wrong."

"No, that doesn't mean something's wrong. Just keep breathing." Anne blew out some puffs and Molly settled into the same tempo as Anne glanced at her watch. "They're about two minutes now, Molly."

"Two minutes!" Cruz kneeled down beside Molly.

"Cruz, I need to get Molly undressed and examine her. Why don't you take John and round up some clean towels? And put on that big soup pot to boil some water so we can sterilize a few basic instruments."

"Instruments?" Cruz said.

"Don't worry; we've got everything we might need." Anne looked at John, who was paralyzed in the doorway. "Use the fireplace, honey. And ask Marta to come in here please. Cruz, you're going to have to take over with Jesse for a few minutes while we figure out what's going on."

"Holy mother, you're not going to try and deliver the baby?" Cruz said. "Molly, I think we should try the road."

"I was an obstetrics nurse for awhile. I know exactly what I'm doing. Now please do what I asked. John, help Cruz with the fire, okay? And make some coffee. But get Marta first."

Molly gasped, and clenched Anne's hand again.

"It's okay, honey, keep breathing."

Cruz and John exchanged looks and hurried off.

# # #

When Anne laid the perfect, squalling baby on her stomach, Molly looked into the child's eyes and was met with an unblinking gaze of wonder.

Tears ran down her cheeks as a new understanding about love exploded inside her. As a child, Molly had feared that she wasn't loved as much as she would have been if she was Norma and Charles Wintz's natural born baby.

But now she knew first-hand that the moment you laid eyes on *your* child, that child was taken immediately into your heart to love, deeply and profoundly, forever, no matter if it was adopted from another or birthed from your own body.

With a moan of relief, Molly reached for the baby girl and held her to her breast. The infant suckled instinctively, trusting the arms that held her.

Molly's insight freed her of the anxiety and fear she'd struggled with and filled her with joy.

Cruz stood gazing at both of them, his face shining with awe over the birth he had assisted with.

Molly glanced at Anne, who looked overcome suddenly by the perfect circle she had been part of in giving life to Molly, and helping Molly bring new life into the world.

"Thank you for everything," Molly murmured, her hand holding the infant's head against her.

The two women's eyes met. "Now you will love as you have been loved," Anne said softly.

Molly's eyes filled with tears that Anne understood this moment, and all that it meant to her.

#

Two hours later, Molly woke from a short nap to find Cruz standing next to her.

"Jesse said we should name her Merry," Cruz smiled. "What do you think?"

Molly grinned and stretched her arms above her head. She let out a rattling sigh and burrowed her head into the pillow. The linen had been changed, along with her clothes, after the birth and she was feeling exhausted but over-the-moon happy. "I like it. It is better than Rudolph. Or Lowly Worm."

Cruz chuckled and rocked the tiny bundle. "Merry is a beautiful name. I am not sure about the M.M. initials, though. What would we use for her middle name?"

"We could make it worse. We could use Marta."

"Or Molly," Cruz said as the baby yawned. "M.M.M."

"Mmmmmmm." Molly giggled. "We are not doing that to this child. We could name her Marianne though. What do you think?"

Cruz nodded. "After your mother."

"After one of my dear mothers." Anne had been calm and competent, coaching her and Cruz, capably handling the last phases of the babe's delivery like the professional nurse she was.

"It's my crowning achievement," Anne said suddenly from the doorway. She walked into the room and stopped beside Cruz. "I think I am going to retire now. Nothing can top this."

"Thank you so much, dear mother of my wife." Cruz's voice cracked.

She patted his shoulder. "Thank you both for doing such a great job. I honestly think you could have handled it yourself with Marta's help."

Marta bustled into the room and immediately shook her head in disagreement. "Oh, holy mother, no. My sister Rosa was a midwife, and I helped her a few times, but I couldn't do what you did, Anne. You're the guardian angel today for this little one." She touched the baby in her son's arms and beamed. "*Chiquita*."

"You're a guardian angel, *once again*." Molly smiled at Anne, both of them remembering how Anne had nursed Norma Wintz through the last days of her cancer.

"I'm sure Norma is watching all of us with a big smile," Anne said.

The baby began to fuss and everyone stared at her.

"You want your momma, little girl?" Cruz asked.

Molly glanced at the clock. It was just after two in the afternoon. Anne said to feed the baby on demand, whenever it wanted to suckle.

Cruz handed the child to her. She pulled her nightgown off her shoulder and took the baby, amazed at the tiny rosebud lips that knew instinctively just want to do.

"We'll finish lunch. Let us know when you want some soup," Marta said.

"In a little while." She turned to Cruz. "Can you bring me some water? I'm parched."

"I'll be right back." Cruz left the room along with the beaming grandmothers and Molly closed her eyes and leaned back.

She reran the day's events. Her labor and delivery had lasted a little more than four hours. How pain like that could be lived through, she didn't understand, but it was already receding in her mind. Probably because seeing her child simply made it all worth it.

She was chubby and pink and had a shock of curly dark hair. Anne estimated the baby weighed about seven pounds, and seemed completely healthy.

She had cried lustily as soon as they had smacked her on the back. Anne had cleared the baby's throat and nose, and put antibiotic drops in each of her eyes.

"She's perfect," Anne said. "But we must get to the hospital later today and let a doctor check Molly and the baby. And get a birth certificate filed."

The storm had died down, but the electricity and cell service was still out. John had driven off to Helen Nunez's to call for an ambulance if Helen's landline was working. If not, he was going to go into Taos and get help.

"Are you hungry yet, *chica?*" Cruz reappeared beside the bed.

She opened her eyes. "No. Just thirsty." She took the glass, drained it, and handed it back to Cruz. "Can you get me a mug of hot tea?"

"Yes." He kissed her on the forehead.

Molly watched her husband walk out of the room. *I have a husband. And a baby!* She sighed. She could not seem to stop doing that. Sighing with happiness. And fatigue. She smiled, knowing those two feelings were sure to be synonymous for a while.

The noises from the kitchen told her Marta and Anne were again feeding everyone while they all celebrated the baby's surprise arrival.

Cruz reappeared with a cup of tea he set beside the bed. He folded his arms over his chest. "Quite a Christmas, *Señora* Morales. What are we doing next year to top this?"

They both laughed.

"Can you take a picture of the three of us," Molly said. "A selfie we can share with our wedding party, since they left before they got to meet this one."

"Yes." He pulled his phone from his pocket and flipped to the camera. "Should we give the photo to the magazine, too? It might mean more money for Helen's school."

"We'll let Celia work something out in a couple of weeks for that, and include a photo that doesn't show my boobs." She straightened her nightgown and moved the sleeping baby to the crook of her arm. "Let's make her first one just for our *familia*."

Cruz nodded and lay down carefully beside Molly on the bed.

With his arm around his wife and new baby, and a tender smile on his face, Cruz snapped their daughter's first photograph.

He held the screen out for Molly to see.

"That's a keeper." Tears of joy filled her eyes. Molly Harper – *actress, wife, and mother* – marveled at how one image had captured the whole, wondrous story of how her life had changed forever the day after a December wedding.

the end

*If you've enjoyed the realism and emotion of the three stories of Molly and Cruz (**DUETS, MOLLY HARPER**, and **DECEMBER WEDDING**) you might enjoy the compelling story of Cathy and Nick Chance in **SECRET SISTER**, Emelle Gamble's novel with a paranormal twist. **SECRET SISTER** won an Honorable Mention in the 2013 InD'tale Magazine RONE AWARDS for Best Contemporary Novel!*

"I wish I were you, Lupeyloo," I said softly.

Roxanne tilted her chin up, surprised by my words, and I caught the shadow of a smile.

This dumb little verse was a line from a school play we'd both seen in middle school, a story about nerdy twelve-year-olds who always want to be someone else. In the script, someone got leukemia or a flesh-eating disease or something, and the kids realize they were special just as they were. The play was hokey, but both of us had remembered the line to great laughter in high school. And we'd said it to one another a hundred times over the years.

Mostly me to her.

Rox tossed her sunglasses into the backseat. "I can't remember the last time you said that to me, Cathy. You wouldn't really want to be me for a second. Would you?"

"I always want to be you. Look at you. Angelina Jolie would want to be you if she was sitting here."

"Don't lie. You never judge people by how they look, but how they treat other people. So fair and kind." Her voice was dreamy, but not particularly happy. "That's why everyone loves you. That's why Nick loves you. Why he's there to watch over you. Believe me, Cathy, it's *me* who would love to be *you*. I really would."

I had never heard such yearning in her voice. "You'll find the *right* man some day, Rox." *A man like Nick.* I kept that thought to myself.

"If I can't have Michael, I'm done with men. All men."

"Don't be crazy." Which was a dumb thing to say. I bit my lip.

"I wish I were you, Lupeyloo." Roxanne laughed then, but it sounded more like a gasp, or a cry.

I turned my eyes back to the road, thinking I should offer to come in with her to talk to Dr. Seth today, if Rox wanted me to. Maybe that would help. We'd done this in the past, given the doc an inside and outside view of Roxanne's aching heart. I opened my mouth to suggest it, but didn't get the words out.

Because that's when I saw the truck.

It was coming directly at us, forty yards ahead. Way, *way* too close. It veered to the middle of the road, as if the driver didn't see us.

I inhaled to scream and grabbed Roxanne's arm, remembering only then that my seatbelt was unfastened.

Roxanne cried out, "Oh my God!"

I thought, *Nick* . . .

about the author

Emelle Gamble was a writer at an early age, bursting with the requisite childhood stories of introspection. These evolved into bad teen poetry and worse short stories. She took her first stab at full length fiction in an adult education writing class when her kids were in bed. As M.L. Gamble, she published several romantic suspense novels with Harlequin.

Always intrigued by the words 'what if', Emelle's books feature an ordinary woman confronted with an *extraordinary* situation.

In 2013, Emelle contracted with Soul Mate Publishing for **SECRET SISTER**, a paranormal romance that won Honorable Mention at the InD'y Tale Magazine RONE AWARDS in Best Contemporary Book of 2013 contest, and **DATING CARY GRANT**, a modern Manhattan fairy tale about a career gal, her estranged husband, and the ghost of a hunky screen idol.

DUETS, the prequel novella that introduces Molly Harper and her family, was published in November, 2013. **MOLLY HARPER**, the follow-on novel, which takes place three years later, was released in January, 2014.

DECEMBER WEDDING is the sequel novella that brings to close the story of actress Molly Harper and Cruz Morales.

Emelle lives in suburban Washington D.C. with her husband, 'Phil–the–fist', her hero of thirty years, and two orange cats, Lucy and Bella. These girls, like all good villains, have their reasons for misbehaving. Her daughter, Olivia, and son, Allen, are happily launched on their own and contributing great things to society, their mother's fondest wish.

get in touch with emelle gamble

Email: emellegamble@aol.com
Website: www.EmelleGamble.com
FaceBook: Author Emelle Gamble
Twitter: @EmelleGamble
Goodreads: http://www.goodreads.com/author/show/7123746.Emelle_Gamble

Secret Sister is now available on Amazon! http://amzn.to/17J2Bn6

Once and Forever, a novella collection, is now available on Amazon! http://amzn.to/1h9fZWv

Duets, a novella, the prequel to **Molly Harper**, on Amazon http://amzn.to/1cagyNa

Molly Harper now available on Amazon http://amzn.to/1a7k8Gx

Dating Cary Grant now available on Amazon http://amzn.to/1iiE8Y0

Please leave a review on Amazon and or Goodreads for any of these books. Emelle Gamble appreciates hearing from readers

Made in the USA
Charleston, SC
01 December 2014